ICE ISLAND

THE LEGEND OF THE WOOLLY CREATURES

Frank Christian DeFazio

ICE ISLAND,
THE LEGEND OF THE WOOLLY CREATURES
Copyright 2012 Frank Christian DeFazio ISBN
978-1506-909-30-1

Published and Distributed by
First Edition Design Publishing, Inc.
October 2012
www.firsteditiondesignpublishing.com

Library of Congress Control Number

2012951094

CHAPTER 1
The Meeting From Russia

It is a rainy and windy day here in the capital, usual weather for the springtime here. This late March in 2012 has me sitting at my desk reminiscing about my youth in Pennsylvania. I used to go out in the rain and look for frogs and salamanders in the field behind my parents' house in my youth. Later in college on days like these I would put on my rain coat and volunteer taking elementary school children on nature hikes in the Allegheny forest of north central Pennsylvania. Now I am forty years old and a doctor and professional here at the Smithsonian institute. It seems these days I have a little more time to sit at my desk and ponder things over. I am in sort of a midlife crisis and yearn for some excitement and adventure. I have been here at the Smithsonian for eleven years now working. Don't get me wrong. I love my work here as a zoologist and scientist of mammals for the institute. But it has been three years since I had an outdoor assignment somewhere in a different country and I miss the excitement. My name is Peter Harrison and I am a single man and never married and totally dedicated to my profession. I on several occasions have explored South America and Africa for new species of mammals. I have even discovered a new species of rodent in South America after a few months of wondering in the Amazon jungle. While doing this I came down with malaria which almost resulted in my death. I realized in my adventures and explorations while in the Amazon that I love being out in the field and discovering new species of wildlife.

Today I have a meeting with my boss Dr. John Klotz at 2:00 pm. He says he has some good news for me. It is 1:45 pm and I am just about done putting into my computer inventory of new specimens sent to the institute from Honduras. Well I am done with my work for today time to go to that meeting down the hall at John Klotz's office.

I enter the first part of his office where his personal secretary is working. "Good morning Miss Gentry. How are you today?"

"Good, take a seat and I'll let Dr. Klotz know you are here." She gets up from her desk and enters his office and closes the door behind her. She reenters the room I am in and tells me that I can now go in and see him.

I enter his room kind of excited and a little nervous. "Good morning John". We go on a first name basis for years now. He responds with a greeting and asks me to take a seat.

"I have some good news for you. Today Dr. Rosita Yorgonavich arrives here to start working with you here at the institute. She is coming from Moscow Russia. She has some confidential information on some sort of sightings on a remote island in the north part of Russia. She plans on being here a few days or so working and briefing you. She requested an expert in the field of mammal identification and I mentioned your name. If you are interested there will be some kind of expedition to this island with her in charge of it.

This is being funded by the Russian government and all expenses paid for your services will be covered by them. She mentioned that the time frame for the expedition will be approximately a month to a month and a half long. I knew you were kind of looking for an outdoor assignment since it's been a few years since your last one. This is why I brought up your name to her." After getting up from his desk and pacing over to where he has a world globe on his book shelf He turned the globe to where Siberia is on the globe. He pointed his finger to an island called Wrangel Island. "Here is Wrangel island. It wasn't discovered until the 1820's. It was surveyed by the Russian military during the early 20th century. It is still occupied by only a few inhabitants and much like it was when it was discovered. Well according to Dr. Rosita Yorgonavich another Russian military survey was conducted there this year and after the survey there was a storm and the ship got spun off its course and ended up going 100 miles northeast of the island through some of the most treacherous ice and iceberg waters known on the planet. Here is where the Russian military vessel and its crew first spotted it." He paused as if waiting for a response from me.

I got up from my seat and walked over to him and looked at the globe. "What is it that they spotted?"

"An island, an uncharted, unmapped island, never discovered before. Not even by satellite technology. The Russian admiral of the vessel was shocked. He along with his crew named it Ice Island." He said this with such great wonder and excitement in his voice. "They sent a small crew to the island and spotted something unusual but that is all I know so far. The crew only stayed a short time because of the harsh conditions and weather and boarded back onto their vessel. The vessel barely made it out of the iceberg infested area and this only happened a few weeks ago. Today this Dr. Rosita Yorgonavich will arrive and we will find out more from her. My question to you is: are you interested in meeting with her and becoming part of this expedition?"

I looked at him with excitement in my eyes. "Yes, I definitely want to be part of this.

Thank you for mentioning my name to her and for this opportunity."

He smiled back at me "Be at your office to meet with her at 4:30 pm today. -I'll see you later." He then extended his hand and shook mine. He then went back behind his desk and sat down.

I looked at the clock on his wall and it was already 3:10 pm. I left his office and said good day to Miss Gentry. I then proceeded back to my office to tidy up a bit.

Once I got back to my office I cleared off my desk. I couldn't stop thinking about this. I reached for my maps that I had in my office. I decided to search for Wrangel Island. I found it and decided to look what would be according to scale a 100 mile northeast distance from there. I saw nothing on the map. I was wondering to myself how big could this island be. How could this not have been discovered? What is on the island? My curiosity is killing me. I found myself obsessing over this.

All of a sudden I hear a knock at my office door. I looked up at the clock and it was 4:32 pm. I immediately said to come on in. To my surprise a tall thin brunette woman opened the door and walked in.

"Good afternoon" I said kind of quickly half out of breath from trying to put my maps away fairly quickly.

"Good afternoon, I am Dr. Rosita Yorgonavich" she said with a slight Russian accent. She walked over toward my desk which I was standing at. She saw some of the maps of northern Russia that I didn't get a chance to put away. "You will not find it on those maps there." she said in a very confident voice. She paused a second "I know you were briefed I was coming and a little about the island that was just discovered. I do have more information about the island and want to discuss this with you. I first must know that you are willing to be part of this team which was organized to do a expedition to this island. If yes, then we can start discussing anything you like about it. You must know that this is strictly confidential and can be discussed with no one until after the expedition is over and we are properly debriefed from the Russian government. The only exception to this is your boss Dr. John Klotz who is aware of all this information."

"Yes, of course. I do want to be part of this expedition." I paused a second. "I am Dr. Peter Harrison. Please sit down. Would you care for a cup of coffee?"

"No thank you, I had a long flight and I am kind of tired and hungry. I quickly got a hotel room downtown here but rushed here because I didn't want to miss our appointment. Sorry if I seem a little out of it." she looks as if she has major jet lag.

"No problem, would you like to get some rest first and possibly meet for a late cocktail to discuss the expedition? Or we could possibly meet early tomorrow morning. Whichever you like?"

"Yes that would be great; tomorrow morning, here at 8:00 am. Would that be good?"

"Great, I'll see you then." I walked her out of my office and watched her walk down the hall and exit the building.

She looked totally different than what I was expecting. Although I did envision her Russian accent accurately. She was much more contemporary in her physical features and quite good looking. I would guess her age to be in her mid-thirties.

I decided to call down to Dr. John Klotz's office to let him know what is going on.

He answered his phone and I briefly let him know that I met with her. I mentioned to him how jet lagged she looked and let him know that I am going to meet with her tomorrow morning here. He already knew because he spoke with her on the phone after she left the building. He told me to call him tomorrow at lunch time around noon.

Well it is around 5:10 pm and I would have usually left a few minutes ago. It has been a long and exciting day. It is time to go catch a cab to my apartment and call it a day.

I arrive at my apartment at around 6:15 pm. I sit down at my kitchen table and look at the local newspaper like I do every evening. I had some left over Chinese food that I put into the microwave and decided to eat that for dinner. After my dinner I decided to do a search for Wrangel Island on my computer. The information that I read about was just what Dr. Klotz had mentioned. Because of the harsh weather conditions that are there in northern Russia I decided to make a list of things that I should bring with. This would be my first expedition to a very cold weather place. I figured on bringing long underwear for sure. I would need a camouflaged winter jacket and pants to blend into the environment. Water proof socks and gloves so I won't get frost bite. Snow boots for sure and the usual toothpaste, toothbrush, deodorant, shaving equipment and some band aids. I'll mention this list to Dr. Yorgonavich tomorrow at our meeting.

It's been a long and exciting day. I go to my room lay in bed and watch about an hour of television. I'm very excited about the meeting tomorrow and the questions that I have seem to be on my mind all night. I think I'll call it an early night even though it's already 10:00 pm.

I hear my alarm go off It's already 6:00 am. I seem to be a little more energized and ready to go this mourning than usual. I jump into the shower and brush my teeth. I change into my best three piece suit and ready to head to the kitchen for some breakfast. By the time I 'm finished breakfast the sun is shining brightly through my kitchen window. It looks like it is going to be a very nice day outside. Well its 7:05 am and time for me to catch my cab to work.

I arrive at my office around 7:50 am. I am a little early and decide to take a seat and wait in my office for Dr. Yorgonavich to arrive.

I hear a knock on my door. It was approximately 8:00 am. I get up and open the door. It was Dr. Yorgonavich and she was carrying some kind of brief case. I told her to come on in and take a seat which she did without hesitation. She seemed more relaxed and probably a lot more recovered from her jet lag.

"Thank you for letting me get some rest yesterday. I brought over some maps and a list of items that we will need for this expedition. The Russian government is also going to supply us winter equipment once we land in Moscow." she said in a direct tone.

She pulls out a map from her brief case and a letter that she hands me. She informs me to read it and that it was in English and that she has a copy that is in Russian. I read it over and it is an international confidential agreement. To sum it up it explains to me not to divulge any of the information given to me or anything that we discover while on the expedition until my return to the United States after the expedition is over. The only exception to this is my boss Dr. Klotz. She informed me he had already signed one of these agreements yesterday. After a few minutes reading the letter I signed it at the bottom agreeing to the terms. I then gave her the letter back which she put into her brief case. She then started to lay out a desk size map onto the top of my desk.

"Let me begin by showing you a detailed map of the southern tip of this Ice Island which was mapped by the Russian military. They only were able to map the southern tip and nothing more. They did come up with an estimate of the total size of the island using binoculars and survey equipment. They estimate the island to be around 20 miles long by about seven miles wide. A little bigger than let's say you're New York City Manhattan Island. Here let me show you." she then leaned over the desk to spread the map all the way out. "By using special far ranging binoculars they were able to see that at the far end of the island there is a mountain range and what appeared to be a possible extinct volcano. The rest of the island is tundra and covered in thick ice. Here on the map is where their ship almost crashed and sank into the ocean covered with icebergs. They managed to send a small crew to the tip of the island right here." She pointed to it on the map. "They were only on the island for about an hour and because of the harsh weather had to return to the ship. They did map this small area of the southern tip. It is approximately five square miles." she paused for a moment. "While exploring that area they carne upon a couple of unusual discoveries. They first spotted some footprints and because of the cold weather they did not have a camera available to take photos of the footprints. One of them later sketched on a piece of paper what the footprints looked like." she then reached over to her brief case and took out a folded up paper. She handed me the folded up paper.

I immediately opened the folded up paper. To my surprise it looked like elephant footprints that this person sketched, to be more exact, mammoth footprints. I kept quiet for a second to see what she would say.

"As you can see this person sketched mammoth footprints that he claims were at least one foot in diameter." Other crew members concurred that's the footprints that they saw as well; they also said they were fairly fresh, maybe one day old.

Well I have got to admit this got me real excited. I could feel my heart starting to beat fast. "I have a lot of questions. But this does look like the footprints of a mammoth." I said this almost out of breath because of my excitement.

She looked at me a minute as if she had more exciting news to tell me. "There was also another bit of information that I am going to share. The surveyor who at this time was looking through his binoculars to the far side of the island saw something. He described it as a large possibly hairy creature but only saw it for a second on a side cliff of a mountain. Then it disappeared behind the cliff He said he only saw it for a few seconds and could not identify what it was because of the harsh winds that were stirring up the snow and making visibility nearly impossible." she paused a second. "The Russian military later retrieved me and briefed me on all of this knowing that I am the leading doctor in Russia on zoology and Biology. They asked me to go on an expedition with them back to the island to search and map the island. They want me to identify any wildlife and record it. I agreed but asked them if I could bring another specialist in the field. One who has experience with wildlife identification and an expert in this field.

Well your name was mentioned when the Russian government did a search for such an expert. They also really wanted the expert advice from the American view point. So we contacted the U.S. state department which connected us to your boss Dr. Klotz and well here we are. So what do you think?

I was astounded and could barely get all the questions that I had in my mind together to ask her. "This is incredible. I don't know where to begin with the questions that I have. Did they see more than one track?"

"Yes, there were many of these and they ted back towards the northern part of the island but the survey team said that the tracks disappeared into the blizzard conditions and that they could no longer follow them." she was then looking as if pondering about some questions of her own.

"Did they notice any type of scat or fur samples or anything else in the area? Did they put some kind of marker down where the tracks are located? How long ago did this happen?" My mind cleared up and the questions just started to pour out of my mouth.

"The survey team did mark where the tracks were located with a Russian flag on a three foot pole. They did not see any scat or fur. This just happened approximately three weeks ago." She was saying this in an excited tone and looked as if she wanted to tell me more. "Two days later the Russian military attempted to do an aerial survey with a military aircraft over the island but the conditions near the island are not just treacherous by sea but have constant blizzards and wind turbulence that an air survey would have caused a crash so they aborted the mission. The weather there seems to be constant blizzards and high winds which gave it its hidden security from modem technology and modern civilization. This is why nobody ever discovered the island."

"Amazing, so what's the plan of action as far as the expedition to this Ice Island goes?" I asked.

"We leave next week from Moscow to an airstrip in north Siberia where we will catch a hop on a ship to the island. This means we leave here in Washington D.C. in four days. So, we need to get things organized quickly and ready to go." she then got up from her seat and walked over to my coffee pot and poured herself a cup of coffee. She was sipping on it and sat back down quietly. She was looking at me as if it were my tum to speak or make some suggestions.

I decided to get up from my seat and pour myself a cup of coffee also. I did this to help make her feel more comfortable and give us a little breather before more discussions begin.

"Are there going to be any other personnel accompanying us on this expedition?" I asked this after about a minute sipping on my coffee. I decided that my initial excitement and adrenaline has calmed down enough to ask questions again.

"Yes, there is going to be a military advisor on board our vessel along with his crew. Once we get to the island there will be a small crew to escort us onto the island. We are going to have to answer to General Sal Klienowski with whatever we find on the island. He is not going to be with us on the island but will be aboard the vessel. The first mate of the vessel Eliaski whose name is Lenin Wergovich will accompany us along with a small crew of low rank military personnel."

She seemed a little nervous when she mentioned General Sal Klienowski's name. I didn't want to make her uncomfortable so I didn't let her see that I noticed that.

"The vessel Eliaski is a civilian ship but the military is contracting it out from Evan Goravich who is the owner and ship captain. I have had the good fortune to have met him already before I came here. I feel as if he is a good man and sincere. He has been all over the Arctic Ocean and the seas off the northern part of Russia and has a good reputation as one of the best ship captains in the region. He has twenty years' experience with his vessel in the harsh and iceberg infested ocean."

She again reached for her briefcase and began taking something out. She laid a piece of paper in front of me with a listing of supplies.

"General Sal Klienowski gave me this list for us. This is a list of supplies that the Russian government is going to give us once we arrive in Moscow. As you can see it has all the winter cloths and gear that we will need. The only items you need are your basic personal items such as toothbrush, shaving equipment, hairbrush, soap, deodorant, shampoo. Everything else will be issued to us. If you need to bring wildlife identification books and a logbook or any field material that is fine." she paused a second. "Do you smoke?"

"No" I kind of looked at her in a puzzling kind of way when she asked me this question.

"Do you mind if I go outside so I can smoke? I know that here in America you cannot smoke in most public buildings." she was hesitant in asking me this.

"I am sorry, I didn't know you smoked. I usually don't let anyone smoke in here but go ahead you can. There is no smoke alarm here in my office." I said in a kind tone of voice.

So, she lit one up and began smoking. I supplied her with a small clay dish for an ashtray. I had it on my shelf and never used it for anything. I started to think about some more questions that I had for her. I had food on my mine even though it was only 10:30 in the morning. The mourning seemed to fly by so quickly. I was wondering if she would like to go to a nearby restaurant for lunch. I went behind my desk where I keep menus from a couple of different restaurants in the area. I slowly walked over to the front of my desk where she was sitting and handed her the menus.

"Here are some menus from some good restaurants in the area. We can go to lunch here in a little bit if you want. There is Italian, Mexican, Chinese, American steak house which ever you prefer." I waited for a response from her.

"American steak house would be great." She said in an enthusiastic way. She put her cigarette out and asked to be excused to use the ladies room. She left my office momentarily.

I decided to call Dr. Klotz's office to let him know what was going on. When I called his secretary Miss Gentry answered the phone and I asked her if he was there. She replied he stepped out and will be back shortly. I told her to leave him a message that I was taking Dr. Rosita Yorgonavich out to lunch and would call him as soon as I got back. She took down the message and said she would get it to him. Dr. Yorgonavich then reentered my office. I went for my jacket on the coat rack and asked her if she was ready. She said yes and we left my office to go catch a cab out in front of the building. We finally flagged down a cab and left for the restaurant. When we arrived it was about 11:15 in the morning. The day was perfect outside. The temperature was in the 70's and it was sunny and no wind outside. This steak house is the best in Washington D.C. and I know she is going to like it. She could not stop commenting on how big and beautiful the restaurant looked from the outside, especially the neon signs.

We entered and immediately a hostess came over to us and then sat us at our seats. The restaurant was only half full of people and usually is like that for lunch. It does however get packed for dinner, at least on the nights that I have come here for dinner. A few minutes later a waitress came over to our table and took our drink orders. Dr.Yorgonavich ordered a white Russian. I saw that she is used to drinking alcoholic beverages for lunch coming from her home country of Russia. I on the other hand don't usually drink alcohol for lunch and normally only once in a while for dinner. Today is an exception for me and I ordered what she ordered to help make her feel comfortable. I looked at my watch on my wrist and it was nearly 12:00 noon time by the time our drinks arrive at our table.

I realized that I was supposed to call Dr. Klotz at 12:00. I decided to excuse myself from the table to go use the men's room. I really only said that so I could use my cell phone to call Dr. Klotz. So I decided to call him from the men's room. Miss Gentry picked up on the second ring and transferred me to Dr. Klotz who picked up on the first ring.

"Hello, I received your message. Take your time at lunch but you and Dr. Yorgonavich meet me in my office at 3:00 this afternoon. By the way how is everything going?" He said this in his usual calm tone.

"It's going well. I'll see you at 3:00. Goodbye" I thought I would keep it brief and didn't want to keep Dr. Yorgonavich waiting too long.

When I returned to our table she was on her second drink. I on the other hand was fine with my first and still had half of it left. I sat back down. We had some small talk about the restaurants here in town and the ones that are in Russia. She really complimented this restaurant and her drinks she had. She liked how diverse the restaurants are here in America. She commented on how she wished her home country had such a diverse selection but also how she liked some of the Russian restaurants in Moscow.

I seemed to be warming her up. I wanted to make her feel as comfortable as she is at home. I hope that I am doing this. She seems to be enjoying herself.

We were having some more small talk and then the waitress came back to take our orders. Dr. Yorgonavich ordered the steak house special and I did the same. We both had a couple more drinks and started to loosen up a bit. Our food arrived at our table. We started to eat. Both of us agreed about how delicious it was. We both then ordered desserts and continued with more small talk about our families. She was telling me about her older relative's involvement in Moscow during World War II and how bad they had suffered. She blended this in with her parent's struggles and her over coming her family's poverty and eventually her getting her degrees from the universities that she went to. Eventually she received top honors from the Russian government and in some circles thought to be the top zoologist and Biologist in all of Russia.

She later began telling me about her studies of the Russian brown bears and their habitats. She did those studies for three years in the field. She later worked for the Moscow zoo for another three years. She currently works for what would be the equivalent to our Smithsonian institute in Moscow which is a museum of natural history. She began telling me about woolly mammoths that were found in Siberia frozen solid under the permafrost of the Siberian tundra. She has had the experience of one such trip to Siberia to help excavate one of these creatures and bring it back to Moscow to put on display. She used hair samples to do DNA analysis along with carbon dating to obtain the age of this frozen creature. She found it to be between 9000 and 10000 years old. She did some major studies at the institute where she works on the possible past migration patterns of these creatures. She informed me of how the last miniature woolly mammoths where on the Wrangel Island in about the year 1700 B.C. than where wiped out possibly by disease or humans. She explained how much smaller they were than the mainland relatives located on the Asian mainland. She mentioned her hope of them being on Ice Island but is skeptical until she sees for herself the footprints and the island.

I enjoyed her informing me of this and already knew most of this because of my own studies at the universities that I went to and my intrigue of the subject. But she did have one thing over me and that is she did excavate and studied an actual specimen of frozen woolly mammoth. This is why I kept quiet and just listened to her about this. She had one heck of a background with all that she has done.

She began informing me about the giant glaciers and icebergs that have kept humans from Ice Island. She believes that the treacherous weather and icebergs may have separated this island from modern time. She believes we are in for a surprise with this expedition and says she has waited a long time for this type of opportunity. I agreed.

Well the waitress brought over the check to us. I grabbed it and paid with my credit card. We got up and proceeded to leave the restaurant to go outside and catch a cab. I looked at my watch and it was already just about 1:00 in the afternoon. I decided to tell her that we were going to meet with

Dr. Klotz at 3:00 today at his office. Until then I informed her that we could go back to my office and discuss the situation and planning some more. She agreed.

Once we arrived back at my office she informed me that she didn't get a chance to go through our natural history museum here at the Smithsonian. She said she would love to see it. Well, my office sits on the basement floor of this museum so I thought it would be great to give her a tour. So, I asked her if i could do this with her. She loved the idea. So we left my office and preceded up to the museum levels. She was blown away by are museum. She didn't ask me many questions during our tour but stopped at every exhibit to read about it. She just every now and then exclaimed how wonderful it was. I could see by her expressions she was fascinated.

Well, my watch indicated that it was close to 3:00 pm. I knew she didn't notice this and we were not even close to finishing the museum tour. But I had to inform her about going to see Dr. Klotz at his office. I promised her to view the rest of the museum tomorrow. She agreed but with some hesitation.

We started walking towards the staircase that leads down to Dr. Klotz's office. On the way there she was discussing some of the fascinating exhibits that we have here at the museum.

We arrive at Dr. Klotz's office and enter the first part of the office where Miss Gentry has her desk. She greets us and comes over from behind her desk to give Dr. Yargonovich a hand shake and hug as if to make her feel part of our work family here. The gesture was taken comfortably by Dr. Yargonovich. Miss Gentry than tells us to take a seat and she would inform Dr. Klotz that we were here. So we both sit down and just relax a little. I saw the clock on the office wall and it was a few minutes before 3:00 which was good.

Miss Gentry enters back into the room we are sitting in and informs us that he will be right with us. After a couple minutes he calls Miss Gentry on the phone and tells her that we can come in now. We get up and enter his office.

"Good Afternoon, Come on in and take a seat. How was your lunch?" He says in his normal calm voice.

"It was great I really like your restaurants here in America." she answers him before I could say anything.

Dr. Klotz then begins asking Dr. Yargonovich questions about Ice Island and the upcoming expedition. Dr. Klotz already knew a lot about Ice Island and the expedition from talking with her on the phone the night before. Dr. Yargonovich went over again some of the topics she discussed with me earlier. Dr. Yargonovich told us that she and I are going to leave for Moscow in a couple of days. She mentioned that we would be gone for at least a month possibly a month and a half. She mentioned to me again that all food and lodging and equipment and gear would be paid for by the Russian government. Dr. Klotz informed me that as with past expeditions that I have went on I would still be in pay status from the Smithsonian institute while over in Russia . Dr. Klotz asked if I could keep in contact with him every couple of weeks to let him know the status of the expedition. Dr. Yargonovich again reminded us both of the confidentiality of this expedition and not to discuss this with anyone until I arrive back in the

USA We all drank some coffee and enjoyed each other's company.

After about an hour at Dr. Klotz's office talking things over with him and having a little fun Dr. Yargonovich and I decided to head back to my office. Once we arrived there we sat down and had some more discussions about the details of the expedition. Dr. Yargonovich told me that we are going to meet General Sal Klienowski in Moscow on our second day upon arriving in Moscow. She told me even though this is not an official military expedition because they are flipping the bill for us that the Russian government and military want to be as equal partners on this expedition. She told me that she never met General Sal Klienowski but has spoken to him on the phone a few times. She informs me of her personal suspicions of not just General Sal Klienowski but of all the Russian military. She says she respects them all but doesn't feel they should be involved in every detail of expeditions such as ours and scientific endeavors. I kept quiet about this opinion but I do agree.

While we were sitting there she told me how she likes how I am and wanted to confide something to me that she didn't tell anyone else about not even her superiors where she works at in Moscow. She asked me if I could keep quiet about what she was about to tell me. I agreed.

She began telling me while she was working in the field studying the Russian brown bears that she came upon a remote village in the Ural Mountains in Siberia. This village was hundreds of miles away from any major town. This village consisted of the Yupik people and their language and there culture. She told me of her studies of their language at the university she attended at how she became one of the only people fluent in their language outside of the Yupik people. She mentioned how basic there village was. It had no electricity, sewer systems, treated water, heating systems nothing modern at all. These people are almost the same as our Eskimos here in Alaska but even more isolated. She informed me that when she arrived at their village alone she was the first outsider that some of the teenagers of the village had ever seen. The elders of the village said that she was the first outsider to visit them in more than twenty years. She mentioned that there were only ninety four people that lived in this village. She told me that since she spoke the language they welcomed her very warmly. She told me they invited her to stay as long as she wanted. She told me that she stayed for approximately two weeks. During those two weeks the Yupik people's elders would gather everyone around a fire and tell stories to the whole village. This was there form of entertainment and they did this for centuries. She told me how she was invited to these stories being told by the elders every evening. Towards the end of her two weeks there she took noticed that all of these stories had some forms of truth to them. She gave me an example of a giant brown bear story. In the villages past one entered the village and started attacking some of the villagers. One of their former elders from a couple of generations ago fought and killed this giant brown bear with only a stone blade. This made the elder a hero and it made for one entertaining story for the village to hear and also entertaining for me to hear. Well the last night I spent in the village I gathered along with the rest of the villagers to hear my last story by the fire. I thought it would be a legend story like the others, little did I realize this legend story got my full attention.

The one telling this story was the village's oldest person who was in his eighties and more less the chief. It was a story about a villager from many years ago that went walrus hunting on one of their canoe like boats into the Arctic Ocean. He got lost at sea for weeks. Eventually he made it back to the village half alive. He spoke of an island that the cold winds blew him to. The islands surrounding sea was covered in massive ice chunks and at certain places frozen solid. He got off his canoe and made it to the island which had a mountain that warmth came from its interior. While there he saw animals that he never seen before. He saw huge furry creatures with two horns coming from their mouths. He saw many different things he never saw before.

Once he got warm enough he made it back to his canoe and eventually back to the village. Once he arrived to the village he sadly died a few days later.

When I heard this legend story I got goose bumps. I knew that from all of the stories that I was hearing during my two weeks there that they were based on actual incidences. I had to speak to the chief about this to see if there was anything more to it and also how long ago this happened. After all the villagers left the campfire I decided to go up to the chief and ask him some more about this story. The chief had a son who was helping him to stand up and to get back to his hut. When I approached the chief's son said that he needed to get the chief back to his hut for some rest. He asked me to come back tomorrow to talk with him. I agreed. He was old and needed his rest. The next morning I went over to the chief's hut where he slept and there were a few villagers gathered in front of the chief's hut. When I inquired what was going on they informed me that he had died in his sleep. I was deeply saddened that I did not get to talk with him. I did see how weak he was the prior night and he could barely walk without help. I stayed an extra night to see his burial. I spoke with his son about the story and he told me that the chief was the last one to know any of the details of that legend and that it died with him.

"You are the first person I ever told this legend story to that I heard from the Yupik people" She said with a look on her face that she trusted me and wanted my opinion. "That is amazing. Lucky to have heard it; however it was unfortunate not to get more details before the chief's death. I am sorry about his death." I didn't know what else to say but the chief's death that night looked as if to have bothered her a little bit. "Maybe just maybe there is some kind of connection to the Yupiks chiefs' story and this expedition we are going on. Do you have anything else on this?"

"Yes, the Yupik people have a few different villages that are within a relatively close distance to the one I was at. The different villages of the Yupik people do share stories with each other when they do there trading with each other. The village to the north of them is located approximately seventy miles north right on the coastline of the Arctic Ocean. This Yupik village is a little bigger and is known to do trades with the village that I was at. It is also located a distance of only one hundred and thirty miles off the coast of Wrangel Island. The villagers there do use canoe like boats to go walrus hunting. I researched all of this information but I didn't visit that coastline village to talk with them." She explained this to me with great enthusiasm.

"Maybe more light will shine on this legend once we see this Ice Island for ourselves." I told her this with some hope in my voice.

Well it was getting late in the day around 5:00 pm. I decided to get ready to leave my office. I asked her to meet me tomorrow here again at 8:00 in the morning. She agreed. We both left my office together and decided to share a taxi. The taxi first dropped off Dr. Yargonovich at her hotel and then proceeded to take me to my apartment.

When I arrived at my apartment I made myself some dinner and read my newspaper. I later went to my bedroom and watched some TV. I fell asleep around 11:00 pm. The next morning I awoke to my alarm and immediately got ready and proceeded to the kitchen for a quick breakfast. Out the door at 7:10 am and grabbed a taxi to get me to work.

Once I arrived at my office it was 7:50 in the morning. Dr. Yargonovich was already there outside my office waiting for me. We greeted each other with a good mourning and I unlocked my office door immediately so we could enter.

Once inside she took a seat. I made us some coffee. We just sat there a few minutes sipping on our coffee. I decided to ask her if she wanted to finish seeing the museum. I asked her if I could escort her through the museum. She agreed. I informed her that yesterday we only saw one quarter of it. She seemed excited about the idea. I excused myself from her and left my office to use the men's room. After that I decided to walk down the hall quickly to see Miss Gentry. Once there I asked her to inform Dr. Klotz with a message that Dr. Yargonovich and I were going to view the rest of the museum today and that if he needs me to call me on my cell phone. I stopped there because I know he usually don't get in till 9:00 am. This museum tour that I am going to take her on is going to take almost the whole day to do. I walk back to my office and Dr. Yargonovich is still drinking her coffee. I decided to sit back down and do the same. I told her that I informed my boss's secretary what we will be up to today. So I informed her to just relax because we are going to take most of the day to tour the museum. She seemed to have a smile and a sparkle in her eye for that. I was trying my best to do a great job in the hospitality department. I figured if we begin this museum tour at 8:30 when it opens we should be done by around 3:30 in the afternoon and then we can come back down to my office.

Well, we finish are coffee and now it is close to 8:30 in the morning and we decide to head upstairs to the museum. When we get upstairs to the museum a security guard comes over to us and I quickly show him my employee identification and he waves us both through to enter the museum. Dr. Yargonovich really wants to start off seeing the mammals of Asia exhibit. So, I decide to take her over there to begin our tour. She and I spend all mourning going through the exhibits. At around noon time we decide to go get some lunch. We walk across the street from the museum and eat at a little pizzeria restaurant which she really enjoyed. We then came back to the museum to view more exhibits and finish our tour. It was around 1:00 in the afternoon when we started with our tour again. The whole time I could tell how fascinated she was about the exhibits. We were having discussions about the exhibits but decided not to talk in public about our upcoming expedition that we were going on.

The day went by quickly. I received a call from Dr. Klotz at around 3:00 pm and I answered it. He told me to make sure we had a good time and enjoy today. He didn't need to see us today. He wanted us to meet with him tomorrow morning at 10:00 pm at his office. I agreed and continued on our tour of the museum.

It was around 3:45 in the afternoon and we just finished our tour of the museum.

She remarked how wonderful it was and we proceeded back down the stairs to my office. We entered my office and I told her about our meeting tomorrow morning with Dr. Klotz at 10:00 am. She began to tell me how tomorrow she was making our reservations for our flights to Moscow for the day after tomorrow and for our hotel reservations in Moscow were we will spend a couple of days before heading to our final destination. She went over our itinerary from once we arrive in Moscow. She mentioned how we are going to stop at the Moscow museum where she works and then we are going to meet with General Sal Klienowski at the Moscow museum for a briefing about the expedition.

Well it was getting late close to 5:00 pm. We both decided to call it a day. We were both exhausted from the long tour of the museum. We decided that tomorrow we would sleep in a little and meet here at my office at 9:00 am.

We both left my office and went outside to catch a cab and shared a ride back to each of our destinations.

Once I arrived at my apartment I decided to call my parents who live back in Pennsylvania and at least let them know what I can. I told them only that I was going to Russia for about a month and a half on a tour with another doctor. They were happy for me and asked for me to let them know when I get back. I agreed to call them when I return. I then ate some dinner and went to my bedroom to watch the news on TV. I fell asleep around 10:30 pm.

The next morning I awoke to my alarm clock a little later than usual because we decided to meet at a later time. It was around 8:10 when I finally jumped into a taxi in front of my apartment. I arrived at my office at 8:45 am. Dr. Yargonovich didn't arrive yet so I decided to prepare us some coffee and just relax at my desk.

She walked into my office at 9:00 am. She sat down and I handed her a coffee. She explained to me that she got up early and went over to the airport to buy our flight tickets. She informed me that we leave tomorrow at 6:30 am. She explained that our itinerary for tomorrow's flight will be us arriving in Frankfort Germany after a ten hour flight than straight into Moscow. She reminded me about bringing my passport and identification along with my personal things. She suggested that today at 10:00 am when we meet with Dr. Klotz that we go over this schedule with him so he knows what time we are leaving tomorrow. I agreed.

Well 10:00 o'clock came around rather fast and we walked down the hall and entered the first part of the office where Miss Gentry has her desk. We greeted her and took a seat. She informed Dr. Klotz that we were there and a few minutes later he called Miss Gentry on the phone and she informed us to go into his office. We entered his office and said our greetings then took our seats. He started telling us how excited he was for us to be able to explore possibly where no modem humans have ever been. He asked if we needed anything for our trip. We informed him that we didn't. Dr. Yargonovich then began telling him about our flight itinerary for tomorrow. She told him that we would be in Moscow for two to three days where we would meet with General Sal Klienowski. She then informed him we would then be going to our Siberian location and then to Ice Island. Dr. Klotz asked if me to call him from Moscow before leaving to Siberia. I told him that I would do that. I jokingly told him not to worry about anything that I was a big boy now. He just laughed. He got up from his desk and shook our hands and wished us good luck on the expedition. He told us to take the remaining part of the day off to do whatever we need to do to get ready. Dr. Yargonovich and I then left his office said goodbye to Miss Gentry and decided to briefly go back to my office.

Once back at my office it was close to 12:15 in the afternoon and we talked a little about what we needed to bring and then about going to get some lunch.

We left and took a taxi to a Chinese restaurant which was only a few blocks away.

We had a great lunch and decided to meet tonight for dinner at this somewhat fancy Italian restaurant. We both had some last minute things that we needed to do so we decided to take separate taxis from the Chinese restaurant.

I took my taxi back to my apartment and decided to take care of some financial obligations and then I packed my suitcase and backpack and then I just chilled out at my apartment for the rest of the afternoon. We were not going to meet at the Italian restaurant until 7:30 at night. I took a little cat nap at around 5:00 pm and woke up at around 7:00 o'clock. I quickly got ready for dinner and then called Dr. Yargonovich and told her that I would pick her up in my taxi at 7:15 if she would like. She agreed and so I picked her up and we went to the Italian restaurant. We had a great dinner and afterwards she informed me that she would meet me at the airport tomorrow morning at 4:30 am. We both took separate taxis again and when I arrived at my apartment it was 10:00 o'clock at night. I dozed off to sleep watching some news on TV. The next morning I wake to the sound of my alarm at 4:00 in the morning. I eat a fast breakfast and gather my belongings and double check everything in my apartment and head outside to get a taxi for the airport.

Once there I spot Dr. Yargonovich and we greet each other with some adventurous excitement in our eyes. We check in and shortly after board our plane. I guess this is the last I'll be here on USA soil for the next month and a half I am excited and filled with thoughts about what I am involved with here. The plane takes off and a peek out the window of the plane once in the air. Well Goodbye for now America, see you soon.

CHAPTER 2
Moscow Arrival

Well, we are here in Frankfurt Germany. We landed a half hour ago and it was one long flight. I now see why Dr. Yorgonavich had such jet lag when she arrived at my office her first day in Washington DC. Anyway, we are heading towards are gate to catch our next flight to Moscow, Russia.

We arrive at our gate and start boarding immediately. Once we boarded we took our seats and took off. We have a few hours before reaching Moscow. I decided to take another nap.

After a few hours in the air we finally are just five minutes from landing in Moscow, Russia. I look out my window on our decent to the runway. I can see the famous St. Basils cathedral. What a magnificent sight to see. The plane puts down the landing gear and we touch the runway. The plane taxis to the terminal and parks. Well, the plane starts unloading the passengers and Dr. Yorgonavich and I make our way off the plane. What a beautiful airport terminal here in Moscow. A lot more people than I expected.

Dr. Yorgonavich starts to speak in Russian to one of the airport terminal workers.

She then tells me to follow her to the baggage claim area.

We get to the baggage claim area and pick our suitcases and luggage up and proceed outside. She makes a call on her cell phone. Since she is speaking in Russian it is hard to understand who and why she is calling. Everyone is speaking in Russian and the only -second- language I know is Spanish. I think I'll be relying on Dr. Yorgonavich more than I thought.

Once she gets off the phone she informs me that she called one of her assistants on her cell phone and he will soon be here to pick us up. She tells me that once he does that she has reservations for us at a nice hotel right across the street from the museum where she works at. She informs me that she got us separate hotel rooms next to each other. She tells me one of the reasons is because she knew that I would need her close by because of the language barrier. She also let me know that there are quite a lot of people who do speak English as a second language here in Moscow. She let me know that she will try to speak in English with people as much as she can so I can follow the conversation along. I told her that I really appreciated that.

Fifteen minutes later I see her assistant pull up to the curb where we are standing. He is a young guy. I would guess in his mid-twenties. Dr. Yorgonavich informs me that his name is Evan. He gets out of his car and helps us load our suitcases and luggage into the vehicle. She then introduces Evan to me and we shake hands. We all get into the vehicle and depart the airport area. Evan and she exchange some small talk about her trip. Evan seems to speak

English fluently. He informs me how much he likes the United States and that he visited there once to New York City a few years ago. He seems to be a very energetic and friendly person and makes me feel very at ease.

After a short ride we arrive at the front entrance of our hotel. The bell hop comes over to our vehicle and takes our luggage into the hotel lobby. Dr. Yorgonavich and I say goodbye to Evan and proceed to check into the hotel at the front counter. Dr. Yorgonavich does all the talking with the receptionist in Russian. After she is done talking and receiving our keys she turns to me and hands me my key to my room. We then follow the bell hop up to the second floor where our rooms are located. After I enter my room and look it over quickly I tip the bell hop in US dollars because I didn't have time to exchange for Russian rubles. My hotel room is excellent and I enjoy the view I have of the city from my window. I do have a small table and two seats here in my room. This could be good to work on and look at maps with Dr. Yorgonavich. I put my things away into the drawers and decide to take a quick shower because of the long flight I just had. I call Dr. Yorgonavich after I get out of the shower and we talk and both decide to just relax and take a nap. It is about 1:00 in the afternoon here in Moscow and Dr. Yorgonavich and I decide to meet here in my room at 5:00 pm and then go get some dinner. Her room is right across the hall from mine.

I hear a knock on my door and quickly wake up from my nap. I glance over at the clock in the room and it is 5:05 pm. I proceed to open the door and it is Dr. Yorgonavich. I invite her into my room. She asks me if I got enough sleep with my nap I had. I nodded that I did. We both take a seat at the table in my room. She informs me that she made reservations at a local Russian restaurant only two blocks from here. She informs me that we are going to walk there because of its close proximity.

We leave my room and head down towards the lobby area and then out of the hotel. We walk a few minutes down the street and arrive at the front entrance of the restaurant. We enter the restaurant and it looks very antique looking inside. There is not that many people eating in there probably only a dozen or so. There is a small bar but only two people are sitting there drinking. We are greeted by a hostess but she speaks in

Russian and I just keep my mouth shut and follow Dr. Yorgonavich. We take a seat and Dr. Yorgonavich informs me that she will interpret the menu for me. The waitress comes over and we order two Russian beers to drink.

After Dr. Yorgonavich explains most of the main dishes on the menu I decide to order a beef stroganoff. This is traditional Russian food as Dr. Yorgonavich explains to me. It is beef chopped up and cooked in with a type of sour cream.

While waiting for our dinner to arrive we sip on our beer and discuss our agenda for tomorrow. Dr. Yorgonavich explains to me that tonight is rest night after dinner but tomorrow is going to be full. She and I are going to meet in the lobby at 8:30 am where we will have a continental breakfast and then head over across the street to her office at the museum. She explains that she would like to give me a tour of her museum and although not as big as the Smithsonian institute it still has some nice exhibits that she wants to show me. This should take a few hours in the morning. She then explains that we have a meeting with General Sal Klienowski at 1:00 pm at her office. He wants to go over some things with us. She then tells me that after 3:00 pm tomorrow she would like to take me on a tour of Moscow for a couple of hours. After all of that tomorrow she would like to take me to dinner at her mother's house in a small town just outside of Moscow. She tells me her mother misses her and invited us over and would like to cook for us and meet me. This agenda sounded terrific and I agreed with her on this with a lot of excitement in my voice.

Our dinner arrives at our table and we both start eating right away. The food is delicious and original. We finish dinner and order some Russian pastry for dessert. It was a very good dinner. Dr. Yorgonavich picks up the check and pays. She informs me that I know longer have to pay for anything. The Russian government is covering all expenses from now on.

We get up from the table and leave the restaurant and walk back to our hotel. We arrive at our hotel at 8:45 pm. We both go back to our separate rooms and call it a night. When I get into my room I put on the television and receive about twelve channels all in Russian. I decide to just go to sleep around 9:30 pm., hopefully by tomorrow I'll be over the jet lag that I have.

The phone rings and I wake up startled not knowing where I am. I pick the phone up and it's my wake up call. I look at the clock in my room and it is 8:00 in the morning. The night flew by and I had a good night's sleep. I jump into the shower and then brush my teeth and change into a nice suit. I start heading down to the lobby area. I get there and Dr.

Yorgonavich is already there having some coffee. I take a seat with her and we exchange a few words of greetings. I go and get some pastries and fruit and a coffee and sit back down with her. The lobby area is full of people at this time and lots of them are taking advantage of the continental breakfast.

We finish our breakfast and start heading out of the hotel and walking across the street to where the museum is and her office. We get inside the museum and she shows her identification to the security officer and he waves her through and I follow. We head to her office which is right there on the first floor. Just by me looking around I could see this was a big museum but not as big as the Smithsonian institute.

We get into her office which is fascinating by itself. It is decorated with woolly mammoth tusks and bones hanging from her ceiling and on her walls. She has pictures of them and woolly rhinos all over the room. She tells me to take a seat. Inform her of my liking of her room and her decorations. She starts to make some coffee and takes a seat herself.

She informs me about the tusks and bones that decorate her office. She tells me that they are all from Siberia. She says that a lot of them have been sent to her from hunters or local villagers over the years. She gets up from her seat and serves me a coffee.

After we finish our coffee she asks me if I was ready to tour the museum. I was ready and excited to see the museums exhibits. We get up from our seats and leave her office. She tells me of her favorite exhibit the one she did DNA testing on. It was a still frozen woolly mammoth which is located in the basement of the museum. It is in a frozen kind of walk through refrigerator exhibit; the only exhibit in the world like this. She tells me that we will view that exhibit last. First she decides to show me the rest of the museum. She continues walking and showing me the museum exhibits and I follow her.

The exhibits that I see are wonderful. There are quite a few ice age exhibits with Neanderthal statues and creatures from that time period. Dr. Yorgonavich's liking of the ice age era seems to have influenced a lot of these exhibits. Anyway, we have toured the whole museum except for the woolly mammoth exhibit in the basement. Once we get to the basement we walk through a decontamination room which blows a lot of air on us with high pressure. We then open a thick refrigerator type door and enter a very cold chamber. What I see is amazing. There is a half covered in ice, frozen woolly mammoth with all its hair intact. It is behind a glass case so as no one can touch it. It looks to be a juvenile. Dr. Yorgonavich explains to me how difficult it was for her to have it removed from the frozen tundra in Siberia. She then had it loaded onto a train headed here to Moscow. She then tells me her exhibit has been on display now for three years. I exclaim my amazement of this exhibit to her. She thanks me for the compliment but exclaims how much she would like to see the real thing alive. I kind of chuckle and agree with her.

It is close to 1:00 pm and we decide to leave this amazing exhibit in the basement and head back to her office. Once we arrive to her office we both take seats and drink some more coffee. After a few minutes in her office there is a knock on her door. She gets up and opens the door. It is General Sal Klienowski and his military bodyguard with him. Dr.

Yorgonavich invites them in. General Sal Klienowski tells the other military person to wait outside the office. From what I could see the bodyguard stood at attention right outside the door. General Sal Klienowski then entered into the office alone and closed the door behind him. Dr. Yorgonavich immediately introduced me to him. He shook my hand and he had a very strong grip. He must have been in his late fifties but still looked very fit. He spoke fluent English and had a very serious demeanor about him.

He took a seat and Dr. Yorgonavich served him a coffee to drink. Dr. Yorgonavich seemed a little uptight in his presence.

"I brought for you and Dr. Harrison the winter gear request forms. Both of you can go tomorrow to the military exchange in the Kremlin circle. There they will issue to both of you the proper winter equipment and gear. They are only open till 1400 hours so don't be late." He said this in a very strict voice almost like giving us orders. He paused for a moment. "Everything is ready to go at our Siberian location. Dr. Harrison and you will fly to a landing strip in Siberia. Once there I will meet both of you at the dock area to board the vessel Eliaski. The landing strip is very close to the dock area. - No more than - two kilometers away. The town's name is Koval and is only populated with less than fifty inhabitants. Here are your boarding passes to get on the aircraft. It is only a six passenger plane and you two are the only ones on the plane. I will be going there before you. I leave tomorrow. Both of you leave the day after tomorrow. I will have my crew prepare everything for your arrival so that we can leave as soon as both of you get there. Tomorrow after you pick up your winter clothing and gear both of you should relax and enjoy the day because your plane leaves early the next morning at 6:00 am. Do either of you have any questions?"

"Is the military crew that will be accompanying Dr. Harrison and myself onto the island have any specialists of any sort?" Dr. Yorgonavich asks with some seriousness in her voice.

"Yes, one of them is a survey and map specialist another is a special forces member to help protect your crew if needed and the last one is a communication specialist who will be communicating back and forth between your crew and us on the vessel. Those will be the three military members accompanying both of you. There will also be the first mate of the vessel Lenin Wergovich accompanying both of you. He is a civilian and volunteered to go." He paused again for a second. "Once your flight arrives in the town of Koval immediately get to the dock area and ask for me. Our vessel the Eliaski is the only vessel that will be at the dock and there will be a guard at the boarding point. Once aboard we leave right away and will be going right past Wrangel Island without stopping and heading in a northeast direction for a few hours until coming to Ice Island. The voyage to Ice Island from Wrangel Island will be unbelievably treacherous and hopefully everything will go smoothly. Just to be up front with both of you there has been a lot of vessels sunk right around Wrangel Island and even more so north of there. These vessels sunk due to the iceberg infested waters and the weather conditions. Statistically one in four vessels sinks in that area. Usually they are smaller ones and have a weaker hull. The Eliaski has a strong hull and a good and experienced captain. I just wanted both of you to know that there is a risk and danger to this expedition and that is the first of the dangers. Another thing both of you need to be aware of is the weather conditions. Both of you must take care and wear all of your winter gear. Becoming frozen or developing frost bite is a real danger. The one member of your crew who is a Special Forces member will help you both in briefing both of you how to prevent frost bite and what to do in these severe conditions. I think and hope everything goes well for us. This is a great opportunity to find out what is on the island and map a new location. Do either of you have any more questions?" He stared at me for a second seeing if I had anything to say.

I stared back at him but really had nothing to say at the time. Dr. Yorgonavich replied that she has nothing more to ask. Dr. Yorgonavich then picked up the boarding passes that he laid on her desk.

"Ah, one more thing, do the best at your job that you two can. Both of you are there do identify and hopefully discover any living things on the island. This is our main goal you know. The footprints and the sighting on the island show of a good indication that there is possibly things on the island that need explanation and identification. The second and lesser goal is to map the island which is being taken care of by the three military members that I am sending with you. Both of you and the crew that is going with you will first land on the island and immediately go and look where the footprints were located and marked. From there take over and do what you two do well. The rest of the team is going to first map out the southern part of the island. When they are through the whole team will go north to that part of the island. While traveling the military members will be mapping out the island. Once your team reaches the north part of the island it becomes mountainous and possibly an extinct volcano lies in the middle of the mountainous valley. Be extra cautious and communicate constantly once you reach the north part of the island. The communication specialist that I am sending with your crew has a strong radio that will communicate just about through any weather conditions and terrain. This is about all I wanted to say to both of you. If neither of you have any more questions than I will leave now and I'll see both of you at the vessel Eliaski in two days from now." He seemed relieved to have told us about the dangers and our assignments.

"General before you go I have one more quick question. What is the time frame of this expedition once we land on Ice Island?" Dr. Yorgonavich asks this at the last minute while he is walking towards the door to leave.

"Good that you ask doctor. Between three to four weeks at the most. It depends on how fast your crew uses its supplies and also on what you people find. We will talk more about that on the vessel Eliaski. Good bye, see both of you in a couple of days." He walks out the door and his bodyguard follows him out of the building.

"Well I'm glad that is over with for today. He is very serious and to tell you the truth makes me a little nervous. Rumor has it when he was a young lieutenant he worked here in Moscow with some of the older Generals who worked with Joseph Stalin. Those Generals were rumored to have been very cruel to the Russian people. It just makes me a little nervous thinking about some of the things he might have done or at least know of that was done." She finally tells me what I already suspected of her being uptight about the General.

"Well don't worry that was a long time ago and I'm sure his past won't interfere with our current expedition." I said this to her to help her overcome her uptightness with him. Although her telling me this makes me a little suspicious of him but I didn't let on that I was.

Since it is only about 2:00 in the afternoon and the Generals meeting was fairly brief we both decide to have another coffee to drink and just sit there and relax for a few minutes.

After we finish our coffee Dr. Yorgonavich suggests that she is ready to take me on a tour of Moscow. I am very excited about this and honored to have this opportunity. She tells me that we can walk a few blocks and then catch a city tour bus that will take us to all the famous sites to see.

We leave her office and head outside the museum and into the city of Moscow towards these tour buses. Once we get to the tour buses location Dr. Yorgonavich purchases two tickets for us and we go on board the bus. We stop at St. Basils cathedral and then proceed to the red square. I get to see many cathedrals and the Kremlin. It was amazing and I took many photos of all these places. It was so great to have Dr. Yorgonavich as a private tour guide. We finish the tour in about three hours and walk back to our hotel.

Once inside we freshen up a little and meet down in the lobby area after about a half hour. Dr. Yorgonavich waves down a taxi and we are off to see her mother for dinner. It takes about forty minutes and we arrive there and get out of the taxi and make our way to the front porch of her mother's house. The house is in a rural area and she has no neighbor's insight. Dr. Yorgonavich rings the door bell and waits. It is around 7:30 in the evening and the sun is setting. It is a beautiful time of the day here.

After a couple of minutes a lady opens the door and speaks in Russian and Dr. Yorgonavich replies and gives her a kiss on the cheek. I would guess the lady to be in her early seventies and in good shape. Dr. Yorgonavich turns to me and tells me to enter. We both go into the house. Dr. Yorgonavich tells me that this is her mother. Dr. Yorgonavich turns to her mother and speaks in Russian. Her mother comes over to me and gives me a hug. Dr. Yorgonavich explains to me that her mother does not speak any English but tells me that her home is my home and how glad she is to meet me. I respond with a thank you and we all walk down a hallway to her kitchen. The room smells great from the cooking that she is doing.

We all sit down and have a great home cooked Russian meal. Afterward Dr. Yorgonavich and her mother and I share stories about are families. I learn a lot about her family history and her father's military service during World War II. Dr. Yorgonavich father just died last year at the age of ninety years old. Dr. Yorgonavich and I stay at her mother's house quite late and it's around 11:30 in the evening before we decide to catch a taxi back to our hotel.

On the way back to our hotel Dr. Yorgonavich and I discuss tomorrow's agenda and I thank her for inviting me to a wonderful evening at her mothers.

Well, we arrive at our hotel and its past midnight. We both decide to call it a night and head to our rooms. We decide to sleep in tomorrow a little later and meet in the lobby at 10:00 am. I go up to my room and go to sleep right away.

The next morning I wake up without the wakeup call at around 9:00 am. It felt good to get a little extra sleep especially coming to my room late last night. I take my shower and call Dr. Yorgonavich at her room. We decide to meet in the lobby at 10:00 am and then we are going to take a taxi to the military exchange to pick up our gear.

I arrive down in the lobby and Dr. Yorgonavich and I eat our breakfast and head out of the hotel and grab a taxi. We arrive at the military exchange at around 10:40 am. We go in and Dr. Yorgonavich hands our equipment request forms to them. The military personnel there have us go into a back changing room and take our measurements for our gear. We get all kinds of winter clothing and equipment issued to us. We even got snow shoes issued to us. After about an hour of getting measured and having our equipment issued to us we finally are done. We decide to load it all into a taxi and take it back to our hotel and then go and get some lunch.

We walk from our hotel to a small cafe close by. We get some delicious roast beef sandwiches. After that we take a stroll through a park close to the museum. Dr. Yorgonavich and I talk a lot about what we should first do upon arriving on the island. We go over some of the details of our mission such as possibly getting hair samples, pictures, and who knows maybe live specimens of some sort. We go and walk to her office at the museum. She wants to stop there one last time before we leave tomorrow. It is early afternoon and we decide to go back to our hotel and just relax for a while. Tonight will be our last dinner here in Moscow and we decide we will have a good-one tonight - because we don't know how the food will be on our expedition.

Once at the hotel I decide to just take a short nap and I asked Dr. Yorgonavich to call me to wake me up for dinner at around 7:00 pm. This nap will be good especially since we will be getting up at 4:30 in the morning to catch our flight.

The afternoon goes by quickly and the next thing I know I hear the phone ring in my room. I get up and answer it and Dr. Yorgonavich lets me know that she made reservations at a nice restaurant. She tells me to meet her in the lobby in twenty minutes. I quickly get ready and head down to the lobby. We grab a taxi from the front of the hotel and head to this restaurant.

Once we arrive at this restaurant we enter it and it is fairly modem looking inside. The hostess sits us down and we order our drinks and then our food. We talk about tomorrow and how we are going to meet in the lobby and check out of the hotel. She admits being a little nervous about what General Sal Klienowski told us about all the vessels that have sunk on voyages in the area where we are heading. I told her that I thought about that also but reassured her that everything is going to be fine. After a while and a few drinks after dinner we decide to head back to our rooms. We both call it an early night at around 9:00 pm.

The alarm goes off and it is 4:15 am. I get up and take a shower and head down to the lobby to meet with Dr. Yorgonavich. Her and I check out of our hotel and grab a quick continental breakfast. We take a taxi to the airport. We arrive there at 5:30 am.

We are the only two passengers on this aircraft. We load our suitcases early and board the aircraft. The pilot introduces himself to us and we prepare for take-off. The pilot tells us that it will be a six hour flight to where we are going. Well, here we go to Siberia. The plane goes down the runway and lifts off the ground. I decide to take a nap and tell Dr. Yorgonavich to wake me up when we get there.

CHAPTER 3
Siberia Docks

Dr. Yorgonavich and I arrive in Siberia. It is a sunny day out and the weather is a little cold. It was a long flight to get to here. There is no airport terminal here so we unload our own suitcases and luggage. There is only a runway here and a small building where the air traffic control tower is. The aircraft that we flew on to get here is the only aircraft that is here. Nobody is here to greet us and we decide to make our way to the small air traffic control building. Once we get to the building we knock on the door and a Russian military soldier answers the door and speaks with Dr. Yorgonavich in Russian. They speak for a few minutes. She informs me that he is going to call the vessel Eliaski and have them send a vehicle to pick us up here. We decide to wait inside the building where it is warm. From the runway here we can see the small village and the vessel Eliaski. It is approximately 500 yards away from where we are here at the air traffic control building. After a few minutes have passed a military vehicle approaches towards the air traffic control building. As it gets closer to our building we can see that General Sal

Klienowski is also in the vehicle on the passenger side.

The vehicle comes to a stop and General Sal Klienowski exit's the vehicle and approaches the building that we are in. He opens the door to the building and sees us and greets us with a handshake and a hello.

"You were right General when you said that this is a remote area. While we were flying over the land for the past three hours I did not see anything that was connected to civilization."'- Dr. Yorgonavich said this with such agreement with General Sal Klienowski about him telling this to her back in Moscow.

"I would not lie to you about this. This is one of the most remote villages in Siberia. We are lucky that this is springtime and there is only a little bit of snow on the ground here. Usually there is a lot more snow on the ground. I will have my driver put your suitcases and luggage into our military vehicle and we will head back to the vessel Eliaski. Dr. Peter Harrison if you need to call your boss Dr. Klotz back in Washington DC I can arrange to have that taken care of at the vessel Eliaski. We have a great communication system that will allow you to contact Dr. Klotz." General Sal Klienowski said this in an unusual cheerful happy tone of voice.

I thanked the General and all of us got into the vehicle and started heading back through the village and towards the vessel Eliaski. Once we got to the front of the vessel the vehicle parked and we all got out. There were two military personnel there that helped carry our suitcases and luggage onto the vessel. The vessel Eliaski looked to be in great shape and was a fairly large vessel. This made me feel a lot more comfortable about our future voyage on this vessel. I could also see that Dr. Yorgonavich felt at ease about the vessel just by her mannerism and her relaxed attitude. While we were boarding the vessel General Sal Klienowski was talking to all of us about the different statistics in regards to the vessel and the crew. He was telling us that there are 40 military personnel aboard and five civilian not including us. He was giving us details about the ships dimensions and structure.

The General excused himself and had one of his lower ranking officers' show us to our rooms and promised to meet with us later on that evening. Before he left us he told us to get some rest because of our jet lag. He said the vessel would not be leaving the dock for another few hours.

Dr. Yorgonavich and I both have cabins right next to each other. After the low ranking officer showed us to our rooms we decided to unpack our suitcases and just relax in our cabins until the General gets back to us. We both decided we do not want to interfere with the General at this time because he seems very busy in preparing the ship for our voyage.

After a little while I wake up to the sound of a knock at my door. It is General Sal Klienowski and he wants to show me around the vessel. I open the cabin door and asked him to come in for a second. I throw my shoes back on and tell General Sal Klienowski that I am ready to see the vessel with him. We then proceed to leave my cabin and head down the corridor towards the second level of the vessel. The General takes me to a communication room that has three military personnel working in the room. He then invites me to contact my boss Dr. Klotz back in

Washington DC by using their communication equipment that is located in this room. I thank the General and he hands me a headphone set with a microphone on it. The three military personnel that are working in this office start to adjust some knobs and communicate in Russian with some operators back in Moscow. Eventually the General asks me for the phone number of my boss Dr. Klotz and I give it to him.

A few minutes later I hear Ms. Gentry voice picking up her phone in her office. I say hello to her and ask her to transfer me through to Dr. Klotz's office. Dr. Klotz picks up his phone and we start talking. He is very excited to hear from me and wonders why I did not call him when I was in Moscow. I let him know that I was very busy when I was in Moscow and apologized for not calling him when I was there. He asked me how everything was going and where I was at the present time. I explained I was here in Siberia on a vessel named Eliaski. I also told him that in the next few hours we were going to leave this small village here in Siberia and head towards Wrangel Island and then towards Ice Island. He asked me to be very careful and to call him when I do get a chance in the near future. I told him everything was fine and that I would definitely call him when I get a chance later on. We discontinued our conversation and I handed back my headphone set to the General and thanked him again. The General explained that Dr. Yorgonavich was sleeping when he knocked on my cabin door and that's why she did not come with us. He asked if I would like to see the rest of the vessel. I agreed I would like to see the vessel and he said that he would personally take me through and show me the rest of it.

We went up to the third floor of the vessel and he showed me where the captain of the boat is and the navigational and steering of the vessel takes place. While we are there the General introduces me to Evan Goravich who is the ship's captain and speaks fluent English as well. The General also introduces me to the first mate Lenin Wergovich who will be accompanying the crew and me to Ice Island once we arrive there. Lenin Wergovich also speaks fluent English. Lenin Wergovich says he will see me at a safety briefing and a couple other briefings later tonight. The captain Evan Goravich says how happy he is to have met me and that he will also see me during these briefings. They both seem very busy at the time and I didn't want to disturb them anymore so me and the General left that area and continued our tour of the vessel.

The General then showed me the rest of the third floor which consisted of four other offices and a Briefing Conference room. There were military personnel in all of these offices and in the conference room. The General then took me to the second floor and showed me the whole second floor which was a lot larger than the third-floor. We saw the dining facility which was located here and he introduced me to the chef who was a civilian. The rest of the floor consisted of mainly cabins for the military personnel and the communication center. There was a small recreational and weight lifting room located here as well. We then went down to the first floor where my cabin is located and this was even a larger floor than the other two. This floor consisted of cabins and offices and was at equal level with the outside of the vessels deck area. The General took me around the deck area and showed me the lifejackets and the six safety boats that were attached to the vessel in case of an emergency. The General then took me to the hull area of this vessel and showed me a huge storage area. This area had all the vessels food storage, medical supply and other supplies located there. The hull area also had the engine room and its crew there. This tour that the General took me on took around an hour and a half to complete. He informed me I had full access to the vessel anywhere I wanted to go on board. I then went back to my cabin because the General had some other things to take care of once I got back to my cabin I decided to knock on Dr. Yorgonavich cabin to see if she was awake yet. She did not answer her cabin door so I presumed that she was still sleeping. I went back into my cabin and decided I also should take a nap. It was only early afternoon and from what I gathered from the ship's captain and the General, Dr. Yorgonavich and myself would be in safety briefings and other briefings later on tonight.

After a couple hours of sleep I hear another knock at my door and this time it is Dr. - Yorgonavich. I answer my cabin door and she asked me if l was hungry and ready to eat yet. I let her know that I am very hungry and we both agreed to go visit the dining facility to get something to eat. She informs me that when I was sleeping she took a walk around the vessel by herself She told me while she was doing this that she did see the General and that the General explained to her that he showed me the vessel on a tour. We both arrive at the dining facility and after briefly speaking with the chef I decide to eat some of the fresh sea bass that the chef has cooked. There are only four other people in the dining facility eating at this time. The chef tells Dr. Yorgonavich that the dining facility is open 24 hours a day and that there is another chef but he is off duty at this time. We are given our food to eat and we take a seat there at the dining facility and start eating. The fresh fish is delicious and so are the vegetables and desserts that we eat there. Dr. Yorgonavich explains to me that while she was talking to the General he told her that we would have our first safety briefing in the main conference room at 6 pm tonight and this would be followed by other briefings until about 11 pm. By the time we finished our dinner it was about 5:45 pm and we were ready to head up to the conference room.

We arrive at the conference room and it is a few minutes before 6 pm. The General is in the room as well as the captain and the first mate and six military personnel. We all take our seats and the General is the first one to go to the podium and start speaking. He begins by introducing each one of us to each other both in English and in Russian. He then states about how important this expedition is and briefly touches on the past expedition that went to Ice Island. He tells all of us that there will be three briefings tonight. He expects these briefings to last to about 11 pm. He explains that the captain will be at the first briefing but the ship did not leave dock yet so the Capt. Will be leaving after the first briefing to go and steer the ship off the dock and do his duties. The ship will be leaving dock at approximately 7:30 pm tonight which is a little bit later than what was expected. This is due because of a last-minute supply that needed to be loaded onto the vessel. The General then calls up to the podium a second Lieut. Who will be giving a safety briefing?

The lieutenant steps up to the podium and introduces himself in English and Russian. He tells us that his safety briefing will last approximately one hour. He begins about talking about the weather conditions and the weather gear that was supplied to us. He explains how to put it on so as not to get frostbite or frozen. He goes on about frostbite and then about icebergs and ice crevices that maybe on the island. He then picks two of his military personnel to show us all about CPR and first aid. They all do an excellent job of showing us this. The hour flies by fairly quickly and the captain excuses himself after this first briefing is over. He leaves in order to prepare to take the vessel out to see. The rest of us stay for the other two briefings that are going to last until 11 pm.

The next briefing touches on survival skills in the wild. The individual that is giving this briefing is the Special Forces member of our crew. He gives his briefing in English and in Russian as well. After about 30 min. into his briefing the ship finally undocks from the dock and heads off towards its destination Ice Island. He finally finishes his briefing after about another hour.

The last and final briefing is on communication systems and signals used in extreme weather conditions. The individual that is giving this briefing is the communication specialist from our crew. During the last briefing, the captain of the vessel returns to the conference room with the rest of us to hear the last briefing. The briefing is over at around 10:45 pm. After the briefing the General introduces all of us crew members to each other and to the captain of the vessel. We all just sit down after the briefings and get to talk to each other and to know each other. We are told by the captain and the General that are vessel will be approaching Wrangel Island in about three hours from now. After we pass Wrangel Island we will be heading towards Ice Island which is approximately another five hours journey to get there. The General explains that be had a long day and that he will be up early in the morning at 6 am before we arrive to Ice Island and excuses himself to go to his cabin to get some sleep. The rest of the crew that will be going onto Ice Island stick around in the conference room and talk for about another hour. We decide to meet for breakfast tomorrow morning at 6 am in the dining facility. We were told by the General that our vessel will be approaching Ice Island between the hours of 7 am and 8 am tomorrow morning. We then decide that we need to get some sleep and we all go back to our cabins and do just that.

When I reach my cabin I'm very tired from the long day that I bad. I basically had a long flight to get to the village and after meeting with the General and touring the vessel and having the three briefings and meeting with all of our crew members I am ready for some good sleep. It is around midnight and before I go to sleep I knock on Dr. Yorgonavich cabin door and when she answers I ask her if she can wake me up tomorrow morning at around 5:30 am. She agrees to do that and asks me how my day went and if everything is okay. I let her know that everything is great and I'm just a little bit nervous about tomorrow. I tell her good night and she does the same with me. I go back to my cabin and go to bed right away. I fall into a deep sleep right away.

To my startle I wake up in my bed from the vessel shaking for a few seconds. I grab my watch that is located on the nightstand next to my bed and it shows that is about 2:30 am. Right after I look at my watch the vessel shakes uncontrollably again for a few seconds. I decide to put my shoes and clothes on and go see what is going on. I leave my cabin and head towards the deck area. When I get out onto the deck area I see a group of six Russian military personnel looking over the side of the vessel. It is pitch black outside and they only have some small flash lights to see over the edge of the vessel. It is too cold outside for me to stay out there on the deck so I decide to head up to the navigation and steering room. Once I get up there, I see the General and the Capt. in their and ask them what is going on. The captain looks fairly busy communicating with some of the crew.

The General decides to answer my question and tells me that everything is fine but the vessel collided with some small icebergs but there was no damage. He tells me the captain told him that the vessel is going to have to slow down the knots that it is doing. The General also tells me that this means that it is going to take a little longer to get to our destination. I thank him for this information and return back down to my cabin. Once I get down to my cabin I see other passengers in the hallway wondering what is going on. I see that Dr. Yorgonavich's Cabin door is open and decide to look in and she is awake and wondering what is going on. I tell her not to be concerned and that I went and talked with the General and the Capt. and they told me that the vessel collided with some small icebergs but that everything is okay. I told her that they also said to me that it's going to- take a little bit longer to get to our destination because the vessel is going to have to slowdown. She thanks me for this information and we both decide to go back to sleep. -

The next time I wake up it is to the sound of a knock on my cabin door. I grab my watch from the nightstand and it reads 5:30 am. I get up and open my cabin door and it is Dr. Yorgonavich. I thanked her for waking me up. I decide to take a hot shower to warm up and I put some of my winter gear on and then I go over and knock on Dr. Yorgonavich cabin door and we both head up to the dining facility. We get to the dining facility at approximately 6 am and sit down with the other crew members. The breakfast is very good and once finished the first mate lets me know that we are running two hours behind because of the choppy seas and icebergs. He tells me that the vessel will not arrive until around 10 am. Our crew which consists of the three Russian military and the first mate and Dr. Yorgonavich and I decide to meet in the conference room at 8:30 am. We decide to meet there so that we can go over any last-minute details and to help each other put our winter gear on and double check each other.

We all decide to go back to our cabins and relax for an hour until we meet in the conference room at 8:30 am. Dr. Yorgonavich and I head back down to our cabins and just relax there.

At 8:30 am we all meet in the conference room and go over each other's equipment and gear and help each other dress and prepare for the harsh weather conditions of Ice Island. At around 9 am the General comes down to the conference room and meets with us. The General wishes all of us good luck and tells us to get ready because we only have about a half an hour until we reach the island. The General lets us know that the vessel will be pulling as close to as 200 yards from the island and our crew will be taking a small powerboat to reach the island. Once we arrive on the island we are on our own. The General informs us that we will be on the island anywhere from 2 to 4 weeks doing what we need to get done.

He informs the communication specialist to keep constant contact with the vessel. The General informs us that only in a life or death emergency situation will we be returning to the vessel before our expedition is over. The General lets us know that if the vessel has to move in order not to be frozen solid into the sea they will communicate that with us. But hopefully the vessel does not have to move for these 2 to 4 weeks. Before the General leaves the conference room he shakes each and every one of our hands. The General then tells us that he will meet us out on the deck in 15 minutes.

Our whole crew is now a little excited and nervous all at the same time. We gather our backpacks and equipment and head out onto the deck of the vessel.

Once on the deck we load all of our equipment onto our powerboat and then we go into our powerboat. The Powerboat is then lowered down into the sea. It is just us crew members on the powerboat and we're a few hundred yards away from the island. What stands in between us and the island is icebergs and very choppy icy water. This is very dangerous going from the vessel to the island in these conditions.

Well here we go. The powerboat is started up and we start heading towards the tip of the southern part of the island. Dr. Yorgonavich and myself tum and look back at the vessel and wave to the General and all that are on the vessel. Because of the freezing weather I'm thinking to myself that I wish I was back on that vessel. The truth is that I'm really excited about this expedition and can't wait to land on the island and get the expedition started.

CHAPTER 4
The Landing on Ice Island

After going through some of the most treacherous seas known to mankind and almost sinking our powerboat a couple of times because of the icebergs and the choppy water we finally land on Ice Island. The whole crew immediately pulls up our boat onto shore and anchors it safely approximately 15 yards from the water's edge. We have a lot of equipment to unload and immediately begin to unload it. We all talk amongst each other and agree to move our equipment in land a few hundred yards and set up our first camp there. This takes approximately an hour for us to do. We all then start helping to put our tents together. We have very large tents that are built for this weather. This takes another two hours to do because of this harsh weather. Once we do have our tents completely up we decide to take a break and let the communication guy set up his communication equipment. There is a little bit of a blizzard outside at this time with snow and high winds. We are glad to be inside our tents and it is quite comfortable inside here. We have two tents set up with one of them being our main communication center and break area and dining facility and the other being our sleeping quarters. We will be here for a few days on the southern part of the island. The military personnel will be mapping the southern part of the island and the first mate, Dr. Yorgonavich and I will be investigating the site where the tracks were first located and also exploring the southern part of the island.

It is midafternoon and we rested for about an hour and a half and the communication specialist has set up his equipment inside the tent. We all decide to meet in that tent and discuss our plans for the rest of the day. The communication specialist decides to test his equipment out and calls back to the vessel and communicates with the General. The communication equipment seems to be working out fine. Lenin Wergovich, Dr Yorgonavich and I decide to put our snowshoes on and try to spot the location of the tracks from the first time that someone came here on the island a few weeks back.

We are also going to be looking for the Russian flag because that was used as a Marker for the spot where the tracks are.

We are outside the front of the tent and start tracking east with our snowshoes on and after about 45 min. we spot a half covered in snow small Russian flag. We go over to where the flag is located and it is obvious that there has been a lot of snow fall since this flag was put there. Lenin Wergovich goes over to the flag and tries to pull it out of the ground but it is frozen solid to the ground and there is no sign of any tracks that may have been there in the past. The snow covered half the flag which means that if there were tracks they are probably 2 or 3 feet under snow. All three of us decide to do a search of the area to look for anything that may give us any clues to the tracks that were here or anything else that we may spot. We track through the snow with our snowshoes on in a circle surrounding where the flag is located for about an hour and we spot nothing unusual. The terrain here is just all snow-covered and flat with no vegetation or anything else for that matter. We decide to track back down to camp to see what is going on.

Once we arrive back to the camp we take our snowshoes off and enter the communication tent. All three of the military personnel are inside this tent at this time. They inform us that they decided to wait till tomorrow to start their mapping of the southern part of the island. It is around 6 pm and we are all starting to get very hungry. We have MRE's to eat which are military meals that are packed in a plastic package and are heated up with hot water and consumed. Anyway, this is what we eat for dinner and what we are going to be eating for the next few weeks. We have a small plastic table in the communication tent where we all sit for dinner and eat.

After dinner we all discuss about where the Russian flag was located and how it was covered halfway in snow and how we could not find any of the past tracks that might've been there. The communication specialist relays this information back to the General on the vessel and the General voices his disappointment in us not being able to find any of the tracks. The General asks for us to call him tomorrow morning at some point. The three military personnel discuss with us about their plans for tomorrow. They have decided to get up around 7 am and start mapping the coastline here in the southern part of the island. They explain to us that this should take them pretty much all day to do and give us a hand radio in case we need to contact them sometime tomorrow. We all decide to meet back here at the tents tomorrow afternoon at 4 pm. Dr. Yorgonavich explains to the three military personnel that we are going to be exploring the southern part of the island and we will be back at the tents at 4 pm. While we're sitting at the table some of us decide to get our log books out and record the happenings of our first day here. The military personnel start a friendly game of cards to pass some of the time. After about two hours of talking and playing cards the whole crew starts to trickle into the tent which is our main sleeping tent and by around 9 pm everyone is in there pretty much going to sleep. We all realize we will have a long day tomorrow and need to conserve our energy for it especially because of the harsh weather conditions.

During this long cold night I must've woke up three or four times because it is pretty cramped in this tent with all six of us sleeping in here and two times I had to relieve myself outside the tent. The three military personnel did wake up around 7 am and prepared to map the southern part of the island. The first mate, Dr. Yorgonavich and I slept a little bit longer and woke up at around 8:30 am. We ate our breakfast together and gathered our equipment and put our snowshoes on and decided to go search the southern part of the island.

Once we were outside the tent we discovered the weather to be snowing and cold.

The temperature outside was in the high 20s and not expected to get past 30 degrees. We decided to start our expedition of the southern part of the island by heading east of where our camp was located. It was very slow moving for us even with the snowshoes on. We must have walked for about an hour and the terrain remained the same. It was flat and totally snow-covered anywhere from 1 foot to 4 feet of snow and it looked like the whole southern part of the island was this way.

The first mate did get out his binoculars and took a look around. He could see in the very far distance the northern part of the island and how it was totally different than the southern part of the island as far as the terrain goes. He told us that it was very mountainous with a large mountain in the middle that looked to be like a volcano. He also said it seemed to be that there was some type of green vegetation or plant life growing on these mountains and near the volcano that was in the middle. He could only see this vaguely through his binoculars. We decided just to continue searching the southern part of the island because the northern part of the island we would get to next week and also because it is a good full day trek from here. We continue our search by going further east for about another hour until we reach the coastline.

While exploring the coastline for a little bit we spot a dead humpback whale that has washed ashore. It was a medium-size female whale and was frozen solid and probably has been on the shore for a few weeks. It was early afternoon by the time we left the shoreline and headed back towards our camp area. We didn't spot anything unusual our first full day of exploring the southern part of the island. We walk for about two hours to get back to our camp and we are all pretty much exhausted from this long day.

The three Russian military personnel did not get back yet from their mapping of the southern part of the island. It is around quarter of four in the afternoon and we decide to wait inside the communication tent for the three Russian military to return. We do have our hand radio on us to communicate with them if need be but decide to give them a little bit more time to return. About another half an hour passes by and they do return and tell us about their exciting mapping of the southern part of the island. They tell us while they were mapping that they saw a huge walrus along the West coast line but that as soon as the walrus saw them it jumped back into the ocean out of sight. We let them know that we saw a dead carcass of a humpback whale but that is all that we saw. The three Russian military personnel let us know that they did call the General on the vessel in the morning before they took off to go mapping.

The communication specialist thinks it's a good idea that they call again to let the General know how the first full day went. We all agree that he should call the General on the vessel.

The Communication specialist calls the vessel and speaks with the General and informs him that the mapping of the southern part of the island is going very well and then passes the microphone headphone set to Dr. Yorgonavich who speaks with the General and tells him about the dead humpback whale that we have spotted and the huge walrus that the military team spotted. The General seemed pleased with the first days effort and asked us to call back tomorrow and let them know what goes on the second day.

The three Russian military personnel, the first mate, Dr. Yorgonavich and myself are getting very hungry and decide to eat there in the communication tent. We all discuss about what we're going to do tomorrow and we come up with a different plan. We all decide that we will leave together tomorrow as one group. We decide that we are going to explore and map the central southern part of the island. We decide that we will get up around 8 am tomorrow morning to do this. All of us decide to get out our logbooks and make our entries into our logbooks for the events of today.

After we finished our dinner it is around 6:30 pm and we decide to have a friendly game of cards there in the communication tent. We play cards for about two hours before deciding to call it a night. Tonight we all end up going into our sleep tent at around the same time. By the time everyone settles in and gets to sleep it is around 9:30 pm. It is another cold night and gets down to about 0°. Our sleeping bags are very thick and comfortable to sleep in and our sleeping tent is fairly cozy. I did sleep through the night a little bit better than the first night. The night goes by very quickly and 8 am arrives. We all get up and get ready to take care of our business.

It is very cold and brisk outside with snow coming down. We all get our snow gear on and are snow shoes and start heading towards the central southern part of the island. We walk along for about an hour and a half and the whole time the Russian military crew are mapping and surveying. So far Dr. Yorgonavich and I have not seen any forms of life whatsoever. We pretty much explore the whole south-central part of the island all day and the military personnel mapped it all out. The only thing that Dr. Yorgonavich and I noticed was a small hill that had what appeared to be possibly some type of old tracks that may have been on top of this hill for a long time. It was kind of hard to tell because the snow covered most of these old tracks and the tracks looked like Frisbee size circles in the snow. There was only about a dozen of these Frisbee sized circles in the snow on top of this hill and was very hard to distinguish if these were tracks at all. This was still a very exciting and significant find.

The first mate took out his specialized snow camera and took pictures of these Frisbee shaped circles. By the time the late afternoon arrived we were done with our third day of exploring the island. We all decided to head back to our camp and when we arrived there it was approximately 5:30 in the afternoon and we decided to go into the communication tent right away and call back to the vessel and let the General know about the Frisbee shaped circles that we saw in the snow. When he heard about this he was very excited and we decided to let him know that we were going to stay one more full day in the southern part of the island and explore it tomorrow. The General agreed that we should stay one more day and explore the southern part of the island before heading to the more mountainous northern part of the island.

The first mate, Lenin Wergovich whet out of the tent to relieve himself. We all walk about 10 yards west of our two tents when we need to relieve ourselves and that is where we go to do this. The first mate came back in kind of startled and wanting to tell us something. He said in a very half out of breath way that he just saw a polar bear when he was relieving himself and that it was about 20 yards from the camp. He said that it did start to run when he got up and that it looked gigantic eight or nine foot polar bear. Well, we all decided to go outside and take a look and see what we could find. We all walked over to where the first mate said he saw this polar bear.

Now the weather was snowing and the wind was blowing but we did not see any polar bear. We did however spot the polar bears foot prints in the snow and saw that he was probably sniffing around where we relieve ourselves and where we put our trash which is in the same location as where we relieve ourselves. This is a pretty incredible find to know that there are polar bears here.

Well it is getting kind of late and is around 6:30 pm and we decided to take some photos of the polar bear tracks and then head back into our tent to eat dinner. We pretty much do the same routine as the night before where we eat dinner and then play some cards afterwards. At around 9 pm we decide to discuss what we're going to do tomorrow as a group. The three military personnel let us know that they pretty much mapped the whole southern part of the island. They're very happy how their mapping and surveying turned out and they showed us the map that they had created of the southern part of the island. I've got to say it was an excellent looking map and could be read very easily and very accurately. They did a very excellent job. We all decided to push ourselves to the center part of the island tomorrow possibly only a mile or two away from where the glaciers and mountains start. This would make us about 2 miles away from what would be considered the northern part of the island. In order for us to do this we are going to have to wake up at about 8:30 in the morning and track about five hours north of our camp past the point that we made it today. It is going to take most of the day tomorrow just to track their and to track back so we decided to kill two birds with one stone and bring some of our supplies from our tent and equipment so that we can leave it right at the foot of the glaciers and the northern part of the island. We are only probably going to be able to explore this part tomorrow for about a half-hour to an hour before having to track back to our camp in the southern part of the island.

We will decide to call it a night and head over to the tent to sleep. We all fall asleep pretty quickly because of our long and exhausting day we had. I did not wake up one time during the middle of this night and slept like a log. I did wake up to the alarm of my wristwatch at 8:30 am and everybody else was waking up to theirs as well. We all got dressed into are snow gear and ate a quick breakfast. We decided to leave both the tents still standing here at our camp but we did decide to take half of the equipment on a snow sled and take it with us to our destination five hours north of here. The three military personnel traveled 10 yards in front of us and the first mate, Dr. Yorgonavich and I followed closely behind. It seemed like forever until we reached our destination and it did take us longer than the five hours then we expected. We arrived at our destination right below the glaciers and the foot of the mountains after about six hours of trekking to get there. We were about 1 mile away from the first glacier and just beyond the glacier the mountains started. The equipment that we brought on a sled with us we decided to leave here and this would be a good place to start our second camp. The three military personnel decided to somewhat organize the equipment that we brought with us so that tomorrow we can set up camp.

The first mate, Dr. Yorgonavich and I decide to take a quick look around right beneath where the glaciers start. We only did this for about a half-hour but what we saw was that it was going to be very treacherous to climb over these glaciers tomorrow to get to where the mountains begin. We could see past the glaciers and the pine forest that began on the mountainsides. We were very excited to see forest growing their but also knew that tomorrow we're going to need ropes to attach to each other to get over these glaciers. These glaciers were at least 100 to 300 feet high and were probably as old as the last Ice Age if not older.

Well it is getting late in the afternoon and we all decide that we need to start tracking back to the first original camp in the southern part of the island and leave this central part of the island for now. We leave our equipment that we brought with us here until tomorrow. We all start tracking back with the military personnel leading the way. It takes us another approximately six hours to get back to our original camp and when we arrive there it is almost 7:30 at night. We are all extremely exhausted from this long track and eat a quick dinner and call it an early night. We all get to sleep at around 8:30 at night. We decide to get up tomorrow morning at seven so that we can get up there a little earlier than we did today.

The next morning comes quickly and we all meet inside the communication tent at approximately 7:00 in the morning. The military communication person decides to call the vessel and talk with the General. He informs the General that we are going to be one more day in the central part of the island. He informs the General that we still need to move our tents and supplies in the southern part to where we will be camping at our second location. The General is excited for us to get moving out of the southern part of the island and to the foothills of the glaciers in the northern part of the island. The communication person informs the General that we will call him once we set up camp at our second location.

We all decide to pack up our tents and supplies and start trekking towards the second camp that we started yesterday. This takes us all day to get up there again. Once we do arrive at the second camp it takes us approximately 2 hours to set up our tents and equipment. Again the communication person decides to call the General let him know that our second camp is completely set up. The General congratulates us and asks to be kept up to date with what we're doing. Our second camp here in the central part of the island is approximately 1 mile away from what we consider the northern part of the island. We can see the giant glaciers not far from us and the mountains that are right there also. We are completely exhausted by our long trek to get here and decide to eat our dinner and call it an early night. We are all completely asleep by 8:30 pm.

The next morning comes quickly and we're all pretty much awake by 8 am. We all decide to meet in the communication tent to eat our breakfast and discuss what we are going to do here our first full day at our new camp site. The three military personnel ask us if it is okay that they survey and map along the ridge of the glaciers so that they can put this on their map before we head into the northern part of the island. Dr. Yorgonavich and myself agree to let the military personnel do that and let them know that we are going to just survey along the foot of these glaciers as well.

Dr. Yorgonavich, Lenin Wergovich and I put our snow clothing on and our snowshoes and head out to survey the glaciers. Since we are only 1 mile from where the glaciers start we will have pretty much the whole day to survey these glaciers. Once we get to the foot of the glaciers we are astonished at how big they are and realize there and then that these are going to be something to cross to get to the mountains themselves. We see that the width of the glaciers are a few hundred yards across and that they are bigger than what we expected them to be. A rough estimate of the height is anywhere from 300 to 600 feet high and we only spot one area of the glacier that comes right down to the normal surface of the land. The rest of the glaciers are sheer cliffs of ice. We think that if any animals or life from the northern part of the island comes down to the southern part of the island the only way they can get here is through this one pass or possibly the coastlines. This was my conclusion that I told to Dr. Yorgonavich. We can all see past where the glaciers are and where the mountains begin. Dr. Yorgonavich and myself have noted to each other the vast difference the southern part of the island is with its tundra and no vegetation and from what we can see the northern part is very mountainous and what appears to be pine forests and possibly other vegetation. The glaciers are what separates these two very distinct topographies. I am very curious about the northern part of the island and can't wait until tomorrow to explore it. We all decide after about three hours of exploring the foothills of the glaciers that it was time to head back to the camp and see what the military personnel came up with.

Once we arrive to the camp the military personnel are already in the communication tent and have already spoke with the General and let him know what's going on. The Special Forces member of the military crew decides to have a briefing with us all. He discusses with us about crossing the glaciers tomorrow and how dangerous it will be. He suggests that the three military personnel tie themselves with rope and lead the expedition and that Dr. Yorgonavich, Lenin Wergovich and myself be tied together so that there are two groups. We would follow a few yards behind the military. He suggests that we all wear our snowshoes obviously but also carry ice picks and walking sticks to poke through the snow-covered glaciers looking for cracks in the top of the glaciers. What he said makes sense. We all know that this is going be a very dangerous part of the expedition. Once we cross these glaciers and get to the mountains will be in better shape to explore and not have to be connected by ropes to each other. We decide to celebrate a little bit and have a pretty nice dinner and talk and plan for tomorrow's crossing over to the northern part of the island. We are going to keep our second camp right where it is for now until we get to explore the mountains a little bit and survey for where we can put a third camp later on.

Before we call it a night the military communication person decides to call the General and let him know that we are going be crossing the glaciers tomorrow morning. The General wishes us all good luck and to be very careful. We all decide to call it an early night again and fall asleep at around 9 pm.

The next morning comes with a small blizzard and we all decide to get up and eat breakfast. The Special Forces member of the military crew doesn't think that the blizzard will cause any other hazards to cross the glaciers because there are always blizzards going on. The military members decide to tie themselves with rope and then we follow the same. Our two separate groups then decide to go to the glaciers and where the lowest point of the glacier is so that we can start crossing it. Lenin Wergovich is pulling our sleigh of equipment with us and the military personnel have their own sleigh of equipment they're pulling. Both of our groups then start heading to the top of the glacier with the military group leading the way. We all have walking sticks and ice picks and look across at the vastness of the width of the glaciers. We guess that it is about 400 yards across the glaciers until we get to the other side were the mountains begin.

We start trekking across the glaciers top: We fall behind the military crew by about 10 or 15 yards and follow their footprints. We get about 150 yards across the width of the glacier when all of a sudden we notice the three military personnel that were tied together disappear right in front of us and vaguely hear them scream and then we hear nothing.

Dr. Yorgonavich shouts to me to hurry up and see what is going on. We all run over to where the military were and stop right there. There was a big crevice that was covered with snow not revealing its true depth and when one of the military personnel stepped on it they went right through it to the bottom of the glacier which is probably 500 feet deep. We believe that they fell to their deaths and are in disbelief about this whole situation. Once one of them fell through it they dragged the other two down with them. Dr. Yorgonavich, Lenin Wergovich and I all start screaming down the crevice to see if we can get them to respond or if there is any type of response. We all only see pitch darkness down this crevice and hear nothing from any of them. We do this for about five or 10 min. with no response from anybody. We have a flare with us that we throw down into the crevice to see if we could see anything at all. The flare just bounces off the sides of the walls of the glacier and out of our sight by the time it hits wherever the bottom is. We are all in shock and disbelief about this and presume only the worst that they have died. We try everything we can to get a response and even throw a rope down as far as we can into the crevice. We stay there for about 35 min. doing this. We have a hand radio with us and decide to call back to the vessel and talk to the General right away. We tell him the whole situation what happened and he is in shock like us. We let him know that we did all we could to try to get some type of response and we decide to push on with the expedition since we're halfway across the glacier. The General agrees but tells us to call as soon as we get back to camp later on.

The three of us push across the rest of the glacier with no additional hazards or hazardous situations occurring to us. We make it to the other side to where the mountains start. We are all in disbelief to what happened to our military crew but just glad to make it off the glacier at that time. We finally made it to the northern part of the island and to where the beginning of the pine forests and the mountains start. We all collapse onto the ground and just lay there for about a half-hour. We're all totally exhausted from this experience and saddened by our loss of life. What lies ahead of us is the northern part of the island with its magnificent mountains and great wonder.

CHAPTER 5
The Mysterious Northern Region

All three of us finally make it to our feet. Lenin Wergovich makes a suggestion that we need to gather as many sticks and twigs as possible so that we can mark our path that we just walked across over the glacier. He makes this suggestion so that when we move back and forth over the glacier we don't fall through any crevices and marking this with the sticks and twigs will give us a clear path to avoid any danger.

We all enter the beginning of the pine forest and start gathering the sticks and twigs. We all load them onto our sleigh that we brought with and eventually we make our way back following our footprints across the glacier and putting sticks and twigs every 10 yards or so apart until we make it all the way back across the glacier again.

All three of us make it back to where our tents are set up at. We go into the tent which had the communications center set up and decide to call back to the vessel using our only walkie talkie that we have. We talk with the General and we all come to the conclusion that we must push forward with our expedition even though we are saddened by our loss of life. We let the General know that we will call him tomorrow morning after we have set up our camp on the other side of the glacier in the pine forest.

We all start to tear down our tents and pack up our remaining supplies that were not lost in the crevice of the glacier. This takes us approximately 3 hours to do and then we head back towards the glacier and cross it again with our supplies with us.

Once we get to the foot of the mountain where the pine forest begins we set our camp up. This is where our camp is going to be-for the next week or two. This is so exciting we are in a totally different ecosystem. We just went from tundra in the southern part of the island which had no or little life there to crossing over the glacier. Now we're in a mountainous pine forest area and who knows what lies on the other side of this mountain where the Valley begins.

Today was a very long day. We are saddened by our loss of life and we had a moment of silence in our tents for the three Russian military personnel that were with us and lost their lives. It is now late in the afternoon and we finish by tidying up our camp and salvaging any of our supplies from the mishap this afternoon.

"Dr. Yorgonavich, would you and Dr. Harrison like a cup of hot tea? Lenin Wergovich asks us with sadness in his voice. It was as though he was still thinking about the deaths of his comrades and just wanted to be of some service to us.

"I certainly would love that and I think Dr. Harrison would like that also." Dr. Yorgonavich replies with kindness and appreciation in her voice.

"Dr. Harrison after our cup of tea I think we should discuss our plans for tomorrows expedition."

All three of us sit there inside the tent at the small table and just sip on our cups of tea for a good 15 minutes. It is around 6 pm and we're going to get ready-to-eat here in about a half hour.

"I think tomorrow morning we should get up around 8 am and explore this side of the mountain and the pine forest and map it out as best as we can. We should keep our eyes out for any unusual plant life or animal life. I think from this point on we should be writing in our logbooks every few hours so that we can compare them at the end of the night and make note of any differences in our logbooks. One of us may overlook a new plant species or animal species so we must document everything as best we can. I don't know for sure but maybe by tomorrow afternoon we can make it to the other side of the mountain and see what's there, if not by the afternoon then for sure the next day."

I said this to Dr. Yorgonavich and Lenin Wergovich with some strong conviction in my voice so as to assert my leadership at this point. I believe someone needed to do this at such a sad time because of the loss of life that happened today. I was thinking to myself that I needed to get the courage to speak like this and I hope it was the right thing to do at this time and I also hope that they took it the right way.

"Yes, I think you're right Dr. Harrison and after we finish our dinner I think we all should get to sleep early so that we can be fresh for tomorrow." Dr. Yorgonavich said this with the kind of support in her voice that helped all of us group together again.

We all sit at the table and eat our dinner together. After dinner we take a little bit of time to write into our logbooks. Then we prepare to go to sleep at around 7:30 pm. This will give us a very good night's sleep and at this time we all need that.

During the middle of the night I had awoken to the sounds of howls from what sounds like more than one wolf. These howls sound very close by to where we are. About a couple of minutes after I awoke Dr. Yorgonavich, Lenin Wergovich also woke up and asked me what that noise was. I explained to them what I thought it was and Dr. Yorgonavich agrees with me but also lets me know that there are no wolves found on any islands north of the main land Russia. We all find this very odd and Lenin Wergovich decides to get out of his sleeping bag to go get his pistol and then returns to his sleeping bag. That Special Forces Russian military member who fell through the glacier yesterday was the only member with an AK-47 and a pistol. Although now I see Lenin Wergovich was smart enough to bring his pistol as well and I am very glad for this, because I don't have any weapon nor does Dr. Yorgonavich.

After a few minutes the howl sounds become more distance and to our relief eventually we don't hear them anymore. We all decide to get back to sleep and do just that.

The following morning comes quickly and we are up by 7 am. We start out by eating a good breakfast and we discuss the wolf noises the prior night and decide to take a look outside after breakfast to see if we can find any tracks or evidence to their presence.

"Well, Dr. Harrison, are you ready to go outside and take a look to see what was out there last night?" Lenin Wergovich asks me with great enthusiasm in his voice.

"I guess I'm as ready as I ever will be." I say this with a little hesitation in my voice because outside it is very windy and a very cold morning out there. My guess would be that it's in the low 20s this morning. We all get dressed and into our winter gear and head outside the tent.

To our amazement we see Wolf tracks 5 yards away from our tent. These tracks are very unusual wolf tracks. As Dr. Yorgonavich noticed right away the tracks that are left there are a lot bigger than the normal gray timber Wolf found on the mainland continent of Russia. Years ago she studied tracks like these made by wolves on the mainland Russia and these are approximately an inch or two larger than the ones she saw on the mainland Russia. That would make these wolves the biggest wolves on planet earth. With tracks like these the wolves would have to weigh between 150 and 225 pounds and around 5 to 6 feet long.

"Thousands of years ago there was a wolf that once roamed Northern Asia that was called the bone crushing Wolf. These wolves would have been around the same size as what we are figuring these wolves to be according to the size of their paw prints. These wolves are now extinct and have been for thousands of years but are related to the modem day gray or Timber wolf. Since we don't have any other proof other than these tracks, we can't jump to any conclusions but we should all take note of this in our logbooks today. It looks like these tracks lead back up over to the other side of the mountain. Maybe after we are done checking this side of the mountain out we can follow those tracks to the other side and see where they lead to." Dr. Yorgonavich said this and although I happen to agree with her I kept quiet. In my mind I think she is real accurate about the tracks possibly being from an extinct wolf species but I'd rather just keep quiet until we can figure out for sure.

All three of us decide to explore this side of the mountain. While we are exploring and walking around this side of the mountain we see that there is no unusual plant life or trees. It takes us all morning to map out this side of the mountain here were our camp is located. We head into our tent and decide to call back to the General and let him know what we did this morning. He is very happy to hear from us and reassures us that we are doing a good job. We let him know that our supplies are fine and we let him know about the tracks and howls that occurred here. We let him know that we will call him tomorrow and let him know what we find on the other side of the mountain. After we eat our lunch we head back outside of our tent and start making our way up the side of the mountain toward the top and following the wolf tracks at the same time. It takes us a good one hour to make it to the top of the mountain and we are exhausted. We do notice the tracks continue down the other side of the mountain but decide to stop here at the top and take a much needed rest.

To our amazement at the top of the mountain we can see down and what we see is a great Valley surrounded by other mountains and the one large mountain that is an extinct volcano or at least it appeared to be extinct while looking through binoculars from the southern part of the island is in fact still active. The truth of the matter is the volcano has a huge hole on the bottom side located right next to the Valley. From this huge hole it appears that there is heat leaking its way to the surface possibly from lava that is found within the whole. All three of us notice that there is no snow in about half the Valley. Where the snow is not located seems to be close to the side where the hole is located on the side of the volcano and on all of the mountains surrounding the valley there seems to be snow from what we can see from where we stand at. So all three of our conclusions is there must be heat being drawn out from the hole on the side of the volcano and this is why that side of the valley does not have any snow on it. The Valley seems really big and there appears to be forests and grasslands located on the other side of this Valley. It is so far down to walk to get to the bottom of the Valley that I think we are going to have to go back to our tent and stay tonight and return tomorrow to explore the valley itself. All three of us are exhausted from the hike to get to the top of this mountain and it is getting late in the afternoon so we make our way back down towards are camp. It is amazing to see this Valley from a top of the mountain and to see that there is actually no snow on half of the Valley is very interesting and all three of us discuss this with great excitement in our voices while making our way back to the camp.

When we get back to our tents at our camp it is very late afternoon. We are still very excited about our discovery of this Valley and the possibilities that it holds. All three of us can't stop talking about it. We decide to call back to the General and inform him what we have found. We only have one walkie-talkie and our communication equipment was lost on the sled that the three military personnel were pulling when they fell through the crevice of the glacier. We still have a full charge on the walkie-talkie and it will probably last us for a few more days. This is very important so we decide to call on the walkie-talkie and the General is very excited about the information we tell him. We did inform him about our communication equipment being lost and he also knows that our walkie-talkie will only last for a few more days. We let the General know that if our walkie-talkie goes dead and we need to continue on with our exploration and we are unable to communicate with each other that we will still have our full two weeks to return to the vessel.

The General is astounded by the information that we tell him about the Valley and the volcano which seems to be giving off heat in the Valley which is causing the temperatures in the Valley to be higher and therefore lacking the snow on half the Valley. The General really wants us to explore this valley thoroughly and to take pictures with our one camera of anything that may be unusual or new to discover. The General expects us to call him tomorrow after we explore for our first full day in the Valley.

After speaking with the General about all this we become very hungry and decide to eat our dinner in the tent. All three of us sit down and relax and talk about our adventures of the day and talk about what we're going to prepare for tomorrow. We eat our delicious MRE for dinner and shortly after that prepare to sleep. We fall asleep at around 8:00 pm and decide to wake up early at around 6 am so we can get an early start and explore the Valley thoroughly tomorrow.

The night passes very quickly and it is already 6 am in the morning. All three of us are slow to wake up and get started but eventually we get moving. We all change into our winter clothes and decide to sit down and eat a quick breakfast before heading into the valley to explore it. We all decide to bring our backpacks with extra supplies in them just in case we arrive back to our tents very late in the afternoon or early evening.

We all start heading up the side of the mountain to get to the top and it takes about one hour to reach the top. When we get to the top we take a little breather which we desperately need. We can see the whole valley from where we're standing at. After a few minutes we decide to start walking down the mountain towards the bottom of the Valley. It takes us a good 45 minutes to get to the bottom of the Valley. When we reach the bottom of the Valley, all three of us notice that there is a rise in the temperature not by a whole lot but by a few degrees. We all decide to stop right there and then and make note of this in our logbooks. Also the pine forests which are on the side of the mountain where are camp is located seems to be thinning out ever since we reached the bottom of the Valley. Dr. Yorgonavich notices some unusual plant species which she believes have been extinct for thousands of years. One of them is the Siline Stenophylla which has been extinct for thousands of years until Dr. Yorgonavich saw it now. She also spots some small brushes and small trees and a particular type of grass that coincidentally

Mammoths used to eat during the Ice Age. All three of us are totally astounded and Dr. Yorgonavich decides to get out of her backpack some sample containers and put samples of each of these plant life into the containers. She also gets out the camera and takes a few pictures. Here in the Valley there seems to be a lot of medium sized grasses and brushes. There are also some tree patches located in between these grasses and brushes.

We all decide to push forward on our journey towards the other side of the valley.

We walk for about an hour and I would guess we traveled around 3 to 5 miles when I noticed a pile of enormous Dung. I called to the others to take a look. Dr. Yorgonavich exclaimed right away that it was mammoth Dung. Lenin Wergovichjust stood there and stared. I agreed that it looked like it came from a mammoth. Again Dr. Yorgonavich takes out a sample container and gathers some of the dung into the container to take with as well as take a few pictures.

The whole time that we have been walking in the Valley, we were looking for those wolf tracks that we spotted the other night. The tracks kind of faded once we got to the top of the mountain a little ways back. We have seen no other proof or evidence of any wolves in the Valley area.

"So, Dr. Yorgonavich what do you think about this dung that I spotted." I asked her with curiosity in my voice.

"I definitely believe that it is from a mammoth and I also think that it is relatively fresh, maybe 24 hours old." Dr. Yorgonavich said with certainty in her voice.

"I'm not certain what this is but we better get moving so that we get to the other side of the valley and see what is there." Lenin Wergovich said with conviction.

"I agree. We better pick the pace up a little bit if we want to see what's on the other side of the valley-today." I said softly agreeing with Lenin Wergovich.

At this point Dr. Yorgonavich got up from her kneeling position because she was gathering a sample of the dung and started leading the expedition forward in the direction of the opposite side of the valley that we did not get to yet.

As we continue towards the other side of the valley we again notice the climate and topography are changing. The temperature is rising again and the vegetation seems to be increasing in its density. To us this is very strange as almost we were heading closer to the equator where the sun nourishes plant life and increases the temperature. This is not the case though and it only makes us believe that we are getting closer to the volcanoes entrance which is causing this strange topography and temperature increase. It is as though we are in a lost Valley in the far northern reaches of our planet which contains plants and the topography that is not supposed to be here. We all suspect again that this is caused by the volcano and are curious if it has been this way for a long period of time.

We continue walking for about another hour and we make our way to a clearing which has long grasses growing there. We can see the volcano from where we are standing and my guess would be that it is just a few miles away. We can see the big hole that is on the side of the volcano and it is facing directly towards us. In between us and the volcano is this large meadow like grassland and it has a large lake which looks like it is not frozen anywhere on it. We all get out our binoculars and take a thorough look through them for about 15 minutes. Dr. Yorgonavich sees with her binoculars a small group of large brown like creatures just to the right of us on the shore of the lake. Lenin Wergovich and I take a look with our binoculars where Dr. Yorgonavich is noticing these creatures. To our amazement we think she spotted what could possibly be a small herd of between four and eight woolly mammoths. We all continue looking through our binoculars for about another 5 minutes when suddenly Lenin Wergovich spots something through his binoculars on the far side of the lake which looks like a woolly rhinoceros. Dr. Yorgonavich and I look through our own binoculars and see the same thing and it clearly looks like a woolly rhino.

We all decide that we need to get closer so that we can take some pictures of what we think is a herd of small woolly mammoths. We start walking towards the right side of the lake and Dr. Yorgonavich has out her camera ready to take pictures of anything of interest while we are walking towards that side of the lake.

It takes us about 10 minutes to get to that side of the lake and when we finally get there we see for sure seven miniatures sized woolly mammoths. We believe only one of them to be a juvenile and the other six are adults. Dr. Yorgonavich is so excited that I think she is about to fall over with excitement. She starts snapping away with her camera taking as many pictures as she can. Lenin Wergovich and I are astonished and very excited. We all are about a couple hundred yards away from these beautiful creatures. These woolly mammoths seem to be smaller than our modem day Indian elephants.

We all decide to move a little bit closer towards where they are at. We have to do this cautiously as so not to scare them. We're kind of moving towards them half scrunched over so as to blend in with the tall grass there in this meadow. We get another 50 yards closer and decide to stop and take some more pictures.

Lenin Wergovich is looking through his binoculars to see if he can see that woolly rhino which we saw on the other side of Lake. He does not spot it again and neither do we so we concentrate on observing the herd of woolly mammoths.

We all decide to get out our logbooks and make note of what we're seeing so we can compare them to each other's logbooks later on. After taking notes in our logbooks we decide to observe the herd as much as we can. We notice that there is some small birds flying in the sky so we take note of this as well. It is hard to tell what species of birds they are but birds are not found this far north so it is a very unusual circumstance. The valley seems to be teeming with life and there is a strange feeling that this is a Valley that time forgot. So far it seems like the creatures and plant life here in the Valley haven't changed for the past tens of thousands of years. It is like stepping back into what 20,000 BC would have been like.

After about a half-hour the small mammoth herd decided to go into the water of the lake and this was fascinating to watch. They went up to about their necks in the water and seemed to be enjoying themselves. We have not touched the water in the lake yet but one can imagine that it is very cold. If we were not in this Valley with the volcano so close the lake would be frozen solid. This shows the difference in the temperature from here in the Valley to outside the Valley.

All three of us decided to take a few more minutes to jot some notes down into our logbooks. We all agreed that these woolly mammoths were some type of sub species that was miniature in size. We talked briefly about how during the course of evolution these woolly mammoths probably became miniature because of the small habitat that they have left here and limited resources.

All three of us decide to get out of our backpacks our miniature size tents and set up these tents so that we can spend the night here. These tents that we have in our backpacks are only one man tents and are very small but will do the trick for tonight.

We want to spend our time as close to these woolly mammoths so as not to lose them this is why we decided to camp here and follow them as much as we can. We are still going to take observations of other creatures that we see in the area but we are excited about these mammoths and observing them for the time being. After about a half an hour we decide to make our way to the other side of the lake and see if we can get close to where we saw the woolly rhino.

When we arrive to the other side of the lake we find the footprints of what appears to have been a woolly rhino that came down to the lake to drink. The tracks of the woolly rhino are very easy to distinguish because they look just like our modem day rhino tracks look like. Here on this side of the lake the grass seems to be fairly high around 6 to 7 feet high. We cannot spot the woolly rhino nor see over the tall grass. We decide to just look around the side of the lake to see if we spot anything unusual. After about 10 minutes we decide to take a break and write into our logbooks about the woolly rhino tracks that we have found.

We are closer now than ever to the volcano and the huge hole is staring at us right into our face. We can visually see all the plant life that has grown around this hole and there is no snow to be seen at all. We all believe that this is the warmest spot that we have been at and guess the temperature to be in the low 50s. We're only a couple hundred yards away from the volcanoes hole and decide to walk towards that area to investigate what is in the hole.

When we arrive at the hole which is at the foot of the volcano we recognize it to be the crater of the volcano. The crater though has settled onto the side and goes down to the level of the Valley. When we look into the crater we notice that there is a river of lava that is flowing beneath the volcano. We can feel the heat from the lava and now definitely understand why the Valley is warmer than outside the Valley. Our conclusion is that this volcano has been alive with lava flowing through it for possibly a long period of time. We think this is why the Valley stayed warm for so many hundreds and possibly thousands of years. It is possible that the plant life and animal life have stayed the same for thousands of years due to this warm climate caused by the lava flow under this volcano and in this Valley. It seems ifs just an ideal climate for these plants to have survived and animals to have flourished that would've been wiped out over time or hunted out over time. This valley seems to have survived the Ice Age and the modem human age.

After about 20 minutes and a dozen or so pictures taken from Dr. Yorgonavich we decide to leave the crater area and head back towards the other side of the lake. We decide to walk around the side of the lake that we did not go to yet to get back to where our tents are.

We walk through a small wooded area near the lake that we did not see yet.

We are right in the middle of the wooded area when we walk right into a bone yard of skeletons from dead mammoths. There must be a dozen to two dozen skeletons of mammoths. We also spot an amazing skeleton of what appears to be a large saber tooth tiger. Dr. Yorgonavich immediately starts taking pictures of this large skeleton of the saber tooth tiger. She decides to take a small bone sample from the animal's rib cage. We are astonished at the saber tooth tiger skeleton. We guess that this skeleton has been here for quite some time and don't know if they are extinct now from this Valley or if there are other ones here. We all discuss why the mammoth's skeletons are here and wonder if this is sort of a bone yard or cemetery or just a place where dying mammoths come to. We are puzzled by this find.

We push forward and leave the area and head back towards the lake shore. Once we get there we follow around the lake until we get to where our tents are at. We look towards the lake again from our camp and can still see the small herd of mammoths along the shoreline. We think that this is their main area where they hang out at. We guess though that they probably travel in the valley in search of different places to eat.

It is starting to get late in the afternoon and we decide to gather some sticks and wood so that we can make a fire. There seems to be plenty of sticks and wood around and we quickly make a large campfire. It is around 6 pm and we see that the herd of mammoth's starts to make their way out of the water and into the wooded area close to the bank of the lake.

All three of us decide to get out of our backpacks the meals that are ready to eat. We start eating our dinner, and right after dinner take a few minutes to compare our log book notes. We continue to keep the campfire burning brightly so as to keep any of the wildlife away from our small little camp that we made here.

The darkness comes quickly and we hope that the night goes by fast. It definitely is not as cold as it would be if we were at our other camp outside the valley. We all can tell the difference in the topography and climate temperature and we are thankful that it is not as cold as the rest of the island is. We decide to get into each of our own personal tents and call it an early evening at around 8:30 pm.

Lenin Wergovich wakes up at around 11:30 pm to put more wood on the fire. Dr. Yorgonavich and I hear him as he gets out of his tent to do this. I call out to Lenin Wergovich to make sure that everything is okay I yell to him to see if he needs any help. He replies back to me that everything is fine and that we have enough wood for the campfire to last us for the rest of the night. He then makes his way back into his tent and we all get back to sleep.

During the early morning hours, I would guess around 4:00 am to my surprise and the others as well we hear some howling. This is not good news and we all call out to each other in our tents to see if we are all okay. Lenin Wergovich lets us know right away that he got his handgun out and assures us not to worry. After a few minutes Lenin Wergovich lets us know he's going to go out of his tent to put some more wood onto the campfire. Dr. Yorgonavich and I remain quiet in our own tents. We notice the large flames starting to pick back up from our campfire which was almost dead and we hear Lenin Wergovich tell us that everything is okay and that the fire is going strong. He lets us know that he is going to go to relieve himself close by here in the forest.

Dr. Yorgonavich and I are very close to the campfire here in our tents. We hear Lenin Wergovich going into the woods about 10 to 15 yards away. We have not heard any howls now for about 20 minutes but what we hear next scares Dr. Yorgonavich and myself almost to death. We here Lenin Wergovich scream like I never heard anybody scream in my life. We hear the Wolf pack attacking him and hear the wolves ripping him to pieces and then fighting and growling amongst the wolves. After about 15 minutes we hear nothing but silence. Our campfire is burning brightly and strong thanks to Lenin Wergovich's selfless act to go out of his tent and put more wood onto the campfire. Dr. Yorgonavich and I are scared beyond belief and I hear her cry from fear. I softly tell her that everything is going to be okay and not to make any noise. I reassure her that we are close enough to the fire that the wolves won't come near us. I'm only hoping in my own mind that I am correct. I also tell her that sunrise is coming soon and that the wolves will be going soon if they haven't already gone.

Sunrise comes at around 5 am and the campfire is still burning brightly. I tell Dr. Yorgonavich to stay put in her tent and that I will go out and check on what happened. Once I get outside my tent the sunlight is out enough that I can see around me. I walk a few yards into the wooded area where we heard Lenin Wergovich last night. The site that I find next is too gruesome to explain to anyone. Lenin Wergovich was ripped apart and eaten by these bone crushing wolves. There is blood everywhere and only a few bones remain. I see the wolf tracks everywhere in the soft ground around the remains of Lenin Wergovich. I find his handgun in all the blood that remains. I pick that up immediately and realize that this handgun is our only protection for us now. I don't see any sign of any wolves and I suspect it's because daylight is here now. I yell back to Dr. Yorgonavich that I am okay and I tell her not to come over to here. She yells back to me in a half crying voice asking what happened and if Lenin Wergovich is okay. I hear in her voice that she is still very upset and needs reassuring so I decide to go back to her tent and explain what happened in a gentle voice to her. I get back to where Dr. Yorgonavich is at her tent and see her wiping away her tears from her eyes. I look at her and calmly tell her that Lenin Wergovich is no longer with us. She then immediately grabs me for a hug and starts crying some more.

After a few minutes and sitting by the fire to warm up a little bit I can see that Dr. Yorgonavich spirit is broken by this tragic event. I also feel it in my heart as well. I make a suggestion that we pack our things into our backpacks and head out of the Valley and back to our main campground that has the communication center tent and call back to the General and let him know that we are going to end the expedition. She looks up at me and agrees but suggests that at least we follow the Western slope of the Valley because we didn't see over there yet. She suggests that we can do this while heading back towards our main camp. This was a very courageous comeback from Dr. Yorgonavich and shows me her fighting spirit.

After packing our things up and also taking Lenin Wergovich belongings we decide to take one last look at the mammoths. We see them gathering around the lake again and this gives me a reassurance in my heart that this expedition was successful. Dr. Yorgonavich and I remained silent while watching the mammoths.

After a few minutes of this observation we decide to start hiking towards the western part of the Valley where we will explore that part of the Valley that we did not explore yet and slowly make our way back to our main campsite. We are both silent and the death of Lenin Wergovich weighs heavily on both of our minds.

We give a couple of minutes of silence for Lenin Wergovich and then eagerly start hiking towards the western slope in the valley. I figure it will take us a couple of hours to reach the bottom of the western slope. Dr. Yorgonavich and myself are walking at a very fast pace and we probably are doing this unconsciously out of fear to what just happened last night. I think we both want to get away from the area where we stayed last night.

"Do you think this expedition was worth it?" Dr. Yorgonavich asks me with sadness in her voice. She is walking at a very fast pace but was still able to ask this question to me.

"Yes" I pause for a second before replying anymore. "There is always loss and pain in anything that is undertaken for the sake of good results in the end." I say this to her half out of breath because of our fast pace that we are walking. I'm hoping that this reply helps to keep her motivated. I can tell that she is a little broken in spirit because of the loss of the lives during this expedition. I'm also a little bit broken in spirit but I know that I must show my leadership skills and try to keep us motivated.

We finally get to the Western slope of the Valley and the temperature decreases a little bit because we are moving further away from the volcano. We both decide to stop for a second and put more of our winter gear back on. After about a 5 minute break we decide to follow the Western slope southward towards where we entered the valley at. This is still a few hours of walking time away.

After walking for about 20 minutes in a southward direction I spot some footprints. These footprints seem to go up the valley slope of the mountain. They are very unusual footprints and kind of look human like but only longer and wider. I call over to Dr Yorgonavich who is about 5 yards behind me to come over real quickly and see what I found. She hurries on over to see what I have to show her. I ask her what she thinks made these footprints. Her eyes open widely and again I can see her spirit lift with excitement and amazement.

"These are the footprints of the Yeti! I've heard of these kinds of footprints being found in Russia close to the Tibetan border. I've never really seen them before but I've seen pictures that villagers have taken of them. I was always skeptical but now that I see these footprints with my own two eyes and know that nobody else is here. I would say that this is the only explanation I can come up with. We must follow these footprints up the side of the mountain to see where they go to." She says this with such excitement in her voice.

We follow the footprints up the side of the mountain for about 50 yards. This is where we see that the footprints lead into a small cave. The entrance to this cave is maybe 10 feet high. I take out my flashlight and turn it on and tell Dr. Yorgonavich to wait outside the cave while I check it out. She agrees but tells me to be careful and not to go into the cave that far. When I enter the cave I notice a strong musky odor. My flashlight is not a very strong one and I can barely see anything in the cave. I walk into the cave about 15 feet and decide to yell hello. The cave must be huge because there is a very loud echo from my yell. After my Echo stops I suddenly hear a loud almost growl like response which comes from deep within the cave. This frightens me and I immediately run out of the cave. When I get out of the cave Dr. Yorgonavich immediately asks me what has happened.

"There is something inside that cave which growled back at me when I yelled hello into the depths of the cave. I do not know what it is but it sounds like it doesn't want me in there. I think we should get out of here now!" I say this to her with such fear in my voice.

"I agree let's go. By the way while you were inside the cave I took some pictures of the footprints and the cave's entrance." She tells me this while turning around and heading back down the slope in a fairly fast pace and with me following right behind her.

We make our way to the bottom of the slope and start heading here in the valley in a south direction. Again we are moving at a very fast pace and discuss our findings there at the cave's entrance. We both think that it possibly was either a yeti or some distant relative of modem-day humans. We are not 100% sure because a lack of evidence but we do know there's something there.

After a couple more hours we finally make it to where we entered the valley and begin our way up the mountain. By the time we get to the top of the mountain we are exhausted and take a break. While we are taking our break we look all the way across the valley from the top of the mountain where we stand and see the volcano and the valley below. The topography again has changed and we are now in the evergreen forests with snow on the ground and the temperature being much colder.

We start making our way down the side of the mountain to where our camp is located and where we crossed over the glacier at.

After about half an hour going down the side of the mountain we finally get to our camp and it is in shambles. We see the wolf tracks all around the camp. The tents have fallen to the ground and it looks like the wolves have gone through all of the stuff probably to get at some of our trash and food scraps. This is not good because we thought we would be able to rest here for the night. Both of us discuss what we should do and we decide to just keep on hiking over the glacier and back to the tundra and get back to the southern part of the island no matter how long it takes us. We don't want to risk the wolves coming back and another confrontation. We decide to leave the tents and almost all of the equipment there and only take our minimum gear with us. I decide to get on the radio and call back to the ship. I make a connection with my hand radio to the ship and let them know that Dr. Yorgonavich and I are okay and that we are heading back towards the ship immediately. As soon as I start hearing a response from the radio dispatcher at the ship our only hand radio goes dead. I believe it was the battery that went dead but it may also be from the cold. This is not a good situation we did not need this to happen. Losing radio contact with the ship only piles up our worries and fears. We put our winter gear and snowshoes on and start trekking across the glacier following the sticks that we put their so that we can make it across safely.

Once we get to the other side of the glacier we can see that there was a blizzard and that the snow accumulated another few inches. The temperature here is very cold and looking up into the sky it is very cloudy and looks as if another blizzard may be happening any time. It is like night and day difference from here to where we were in the inside of the Valley. There is no vegetation insight and it is complete tundra from here to the southern part of the island. Walking here is at a very slow pace because of having to use these snowshoes to walk through the deep snow. In the valley there was no snow or very little of it because of the heat generated from the volcano and we could really walk at a very fast pace and make good time where we were going to. We are doing pretty good though walking with these snowshoes and making our way across the tundra. I can see that Dr. Yorgonavich is relieved to be heading back towards the southern part of the island and eventually to our ship. I myself am pleased to be doing the same and just hope we can make it back without any other problems occurring. I also believe that we are going to have to hike it through some of the nighttime just to get back to the southern tip of the island where are boat is located. I am a little bit worried because at night it gets very cold here in the southern half of the island. We do have a couple of MRE's in our backpacks so that when we get hungry later we can eat but it is still going to be very hard to just stop and eat right there in the tundra with the cold. I just think that we are in survival mode right now and will do anything we have to do to survive. This is all going through my mind but I don't think that Dr. Yorgonavich is as worried as I am right now. I just hope that I'm not showing my fear so that I don't make her worry as well.

We have many hours in front of us to travel to get to the southern tip of the island. After about walking almost three hours Dr. Yorgonavich turns to me and tells me she needs a rest and something to eat. I was thinking to myself that I was hoping that we could go a little bit further without having to stop and eat something. I did not let her know that I was thinking this. I just turned to her and agreed with her and then we both decided to sit down and take our backpacks off and take out a couple of MRE's to eat. I was very hungry and so was Dr. Yorgonavich. We opened up our MRE's and started eating our meals without even having to warm them up. I finished mine in record time it probably only took me four minutes to eat everything in my MRE. Dr. Yorgonavich finished just a couple minutes after I did. We are both burning up a lot of calories walking in this extreme cold weather and it was good to get some food in our system. I turned to her after we were done eating and told her that were going to get up and leave in five minutes. I also told her that we need to keep moving so as not to get frostbite or hyperthermia from cooling down too much. She looked at me with exhaustion in her face and agreed with me.

Once we got up from our break we immediately started to walk at a very fast pace with our snowshoes on. I think that Dr Yorgonavich realizes the severity of our situation now and is not saying very much to me but seems to be concentrating on saving her energy and walking a fast pace. After about an hour of walking the snow starts coming down fairly heavily and this isn't something I was hoping would happen. We both just keep pushing on and realize shortly that is going to be nighttime very soon. I occasionally look up in the far distance ahead of me and see nothing but the snow coming down.

After a few more hours of trekking through the snow we stop for a few minutes break and it is pitch black out and I had to turn my flashlight on. The temperature has dropped dramatically and we're feeling the effects of that. Dr. Yorgonavich turns to me and says in desperation that she cannot go on anymore and wants to just sleep here. She falls to the ground and just sits there. I immediately get a little angry and tell her to get up and that we need to keep moving. I inform her that if she falls asleep now she might get hypothermia and die. While I was saying all of this to her and when she did get up I was thinking to myself that I just wanted to fall down and lay there to. I just forced myself to push forward and Dr. Yorgonavich followed me.

This is starting to tum into a game of pure survival and nothing more. It is no longer an adventure nor a scientific research quest. I think we both realize this now. I am guesstimating in my head that we are only a few hours more from where we landed on the island at. We need to make it to our small little boat that we pulled up onto the shore and retrieve the flares that are in their and set them off so that the crew from the ship can see us.

We walked in the blizzard conditions for another 2 to 3 more hours with only one 10 minute break. Even though I have my heavy gloves on and my heavy snow boots my hands and feet are both frozen and I believe are on the verge of getting frostbite. Because of my fast-paced walk I didn't even bother to ask Dr. Yorgonavich bow her hands and feet are doing. I don't have the energy to even really speak at this point. I believe that it is after midnight now and we basically have been walking all day.

Just as I was ready to give up on everything I see through the blizzard conditions the small boat that we came over to the island on. The boat is only about 20 yards in front of us and 5 yards past the boat is the ocean. Dr. Yorgonavich yells to me that she sees the boat. We both put our last bit of energy into walking as fast as we can towards that boat and when we get there we both fall into it because of total exhaustion. I immediately reach for the flares and set one of them off right above us. I grab a second one and secure to the shoreline right near our boat. I look out into the ocean to where our ship is at and I do notice that some of the crew are loading up onto another side boat and lowering it into the ocean to come and get us. I sit back down into our boat and I inform Dr. Yorgonavich that help is on the way. She slides over to me and hugs me and doesn't let me go.

About 15 minutes later I see them coming to shore and walking towards us. It is three Russian military personnel. They make their way over to our small boat and help us to our feet. They help Dr. Yorgonavich and myself to their small boat. Dr. Yorgonavich turns to me and smiles and tells me now that she knows everything is going to be okay. She tells me this in a half conscious state and I am listening to her in a half unconscious state. I am just so glad that we're rescued and made it back. We got to the ship and they started rising our little boat up to the main ship. That is when I knew everything was going to be okay.

CHAPTER 6
The Return Voyage

Once our rescue boat makes it to the deck of the vessel Eliaski I see the medical team with two stretchers standing by to assist us. This is a good thing because I don't think Dr. Yorgonavich and I have the strength to walk on our own 2 feet without assistance. So the medical team puts Dr. Yorgonavich and myself on the stretchers and carries us to the medical cabin. When we arrive to the medical cabin there is a military medical doctor there to greet us. He notices that Dr. Yorgonavich and I are extremely exhausted and just asks us a couple questions pertaining to our Limbs to see if we have frostbite or hyperthermia. He then tells us that he's going to have his assistant come in and remove our clothing and give us our smocks to where. He thinks that we're okay and do not have any type of frostbite or hypothermia by the way we answered our questions that he asked us. He tells us to get plenty of rest and that he will check us in another seven hours from now. He also lets us know that General Klienowski will come back with him in the seven hours to briefly speak with them. Dr. Yorgonavich and I both have separate beds there inside the medical cabin. The doctor's assistant comes in and helps both of us get into our smocks he leaves the room with all of our winter gear and cloths and closes the door behind him.

While lying in my bed I turn to Dr. Yorgonavich in a half unconscious state because of my exhaustion and tell her not to mention to anyone about possibly seeing a yeti or Neanderthal or whatever was in that cave. She looks to me and agrees not to say anything about that. I then see her close her eyes and fall asleep. I was thinking about not telling anyone about the yeti or the Neanderthal that we heard and saw the footprints of not just because we didn't have solid proof but because we are dealing with the Russian military and I don't know what they would think about something like that. I think I was thinking that they may want to go in and somehow capture or kill the creature. I am totally exhausted now and fall right asleep without any hesitation.

I hear a loud knock at the door and it wakes me up. To my surprise seven hours have passed already and I only woke up because of the door opening and the knock. I see Dr. Yorgonavich wake up as well. The Russian military doctor walks in and right behind him is General Klienowski. The doctor right away asks us how we are feeling and if we had enough rest. I look at him and just shake my head yes. Dr. Yorgonavich answers him with a yes. He then comes over to me with a stethoscope and checks my heart and breathing and says that everything is okay. He walks over to Dr. Yorgonavich and does the same and tells her she is fine as well. After that General Klienowski asks the military doctor to leave the room and he complies. General Klienowski turns to us and congratulates us and thanks us for a job well done.

"I am truly sorry for the loss of life during this expedition to the island and I hope that you are all tine. I really would like to hear everything that you have to tell me that happened there. This was truly a remarkable find and I just want you to know that both of you are part of history because of this expedition. I still see that you look tired and that is understandable. I will let you get some more rest and when you feel like it you both can go back to your cabins. I will talk to you later this afternoon during what I call a debriefing of this expedition and also a briefing from both of you two about what happened and what you all saw and experienced there. Well if you don't have any questions for me right now I'll let you get some more rest and I'll talk to both of you later." The General said all this with sincerity but also like he was holding something back from us.

He turned and opened the door and was ready to head out when Dr. Yorgonavich started to ask him a question.

"General Klienowski, I was just wondering where is mine and Dr. Harrison's logbooks and camera?" Dr. Yorgonavich asks him this in a calm voice.

"Well I have them. I am looking over them right now with a couple other officers of mine and we are trying to get the film developed that was inside the camera that you took the pictures with. At the debriefing we may give you back the logbooks and the pictures if we develop them from the camera." The General says this in an arrogant kind of way.

"These are our private notes in our logbook and I don't think you had a right to take these. I would like mine back and Dr. Harrison's back right away!" Dr. Yorgonavich yells this at General Klienowski.

"Listen, Dr. Yorgonavich I think you forget who is running this expedition and who is paying for all of the funding for this. I am a military General and it is my responsibility to make sure that the government is safe from any possible dangers that may have been on this island. That is why I took your logbooks and like I said if me and my officers check out everything in the log books and everything is okay we will give them back to you at the debriefing. Now, if that is all I will let you get some rest and I will be going." The General closes the door quickly behind him and seems to be a little bit upset with Dr. Yorgonavich 's question to him.

"I could tell by the sound in his voice that he wasn't telling us everything. For now don't try to get him upset or mad. Just remember what I told you earlier. Don't say anything about the yeti or whatever that was in the cave. If they do develop the film they're going to see the pictures of everything that we took. If they come to that yeti footprint picture and ask us what that is we can tell them that it was a bear track. The reason I don't want them to know right now about the creature in the cave is just what I thought that came out of his mouth. You heard him. He wants to protect the government from any danger. I just don't want them to think that this creature is a danger because we both know that it's not. I would really feel guilty if they sent the military in there just to kill this creature because of it being a possible danger to the Russian government. Do you see what I'm getting at here?" I tell her this with sternness in my voice. I think she will understand because we are both scientists and want to protect and study not kill anything.

"I do see your point and agree 100% with you. I think with all the other pictures and photographs and evidence we can make a stand to protect this area so that later it can be studied. I will definitely keep quiet about whatever we heard there in the cave." She says this in a very calm voice and agreeing with me.

We both get out of bed and start changing out of our smocks and putting on some khaki shirt and pants that the assistant must've brought to us while we were sleeping. We both decide to go back to our cabins and just wait there until we are called for to go to the debriefing.

The General again thanks us and informs us that this expedition will be dedicated to the memory of his three Russian soldiers and Lenin Wergovich. He is sorry though that he has to keep the log books and pictures for now. The General informs us that his commanding General back in Moscow would like his expert opinion on the matter. His commanding officer would like to see the logbooks and the pictures as well. He informs us though that when he is done showing them to his commanding officer back in Moscow that he will ask his commanding officer if he can give them back to us. If his commanding officer agrees to give them back to us that he will. I look over to Dr. Yorgonavich and see anger in her face. She does keep her cool though and doesn't say anything back to the General. He informs us that we're almost at the dock where we left from before the expedition. He says that we can go back to our cabins and prepare to get off at the dock. He lets us know that there will be a plane that takes us back to Moscow. He informs us that we will see him back in Moscow and that he will contact Dr. Yorgonavich at the museum there in Moscow. Dr. Yorgonavich and I stand up from the table and thank all the people on the panel there. We then leave the room to go back to our cabins.

Once we arrive to our cabins we both quickly pack our suitcases and backpacks and prepare for the ship to dock. Once we feel the ship dock we quickly hurry off the ship. We make our way quickly to the runway where we see a lone single small aircraft there and we make our way over towards it. The pilot gets out of the small aircraft and talks to Dr. Yorgonavich in Russian. After they're finished talking she informs me this is the aircraft that we are going to be taking back to Moscow and then we decide to load our suitcases and backpacks onto it. We both get onto the plane and are glad to get away from all the military and be heading back to Moscow. The plane takes off down the runway and Dr. Yorgonavich and I take one last look out the planes window. This has been amazing. Well I find myself getting drowsy from the plane and decide to doze off.

CHAPTER 7
The Debrief in Moscow

I feel someone shaking my shoulder. I suddenly wake up from a deep sleep. It was Dr. Yorgonavich shaking my shoulder to wake me up. She tells me that our plane is about to land here in Moscow. I look out the plane window and can see all of Moscow. I slept that whole trip on the plane. It only seemed like a few minutes that I was asleep.

Our planes landing gear touches the runway. It sure feels good to be back here in Moscow. I'm curious what is going to happen here in the Moscow Museum. I look over to Dr. Yorgonavich and she seems fairly excited to be landing back here as well. The plane pulls up to the terminal and we exit off the plane. Dr. Yorgonavich's assistant Evan greets us at the terminal. He has a cart with him so that we can load our luggage onto it. Dr. Yorgonavich gives him a little hug and says something to him in Russian.

Dr. Yorgonavich turns to me and tells me that when I was sleeping on the plane she made a phone call with her cell phone to Evan and told him to meet us here at the terminal. I turn to Evan and thank him for being here to meet us. He helps us by pushing the cart full of our luggage to where he parked his vehicle at. He then loads up our luggage into the trunk of his vehicle and drives us towards the Moscow Museum.

Once we arrive in front of the Moscow Museum Dr. Yorgonavich asks Evan to pull into the hotel right across the street from the Moscow Museum. Evan helps us unload our luggage at the hotel lobby and talks a couple seconds with Dr. Yorgonavich in Russian. He then gets back into his vehicle and waves bye to us. The bellhop from the hotel helps us take our luggage into the lobby area to check in. Dr. Yorgonavich tells me that we will meet up with Evan tomorrow at the Museum. She informed me that right now we're just going to check into the hotel and relax for the rest of the afternoon and evening.

We check-in at the hotel and each receives a separate room next to each other on the second floor. We follow the bellhop to the second floor and into our rooms. Dr. Yorgonavich informs me that she'll call me at 6 pm so that we can go get some dinner. I looked at my watch to see what time it was and it was approximately 1 P.M. here in Moscow. I decide to take another nap until 6 pm comes.

I wake up from the ringing of the phone in my room. I answer it and it is Dr. Yorgonavich and she informs me that she will meet me down in the lobby in 5 minutes so we can go get some dinner. I quick get up from the bed and go into the bathroom to wash my face and then head down to the lobby to meet with her.

Once I get to the lobby we talk and decide to go to one of the restaurants that is close by and within walking distance. We leave the hotel and walk across the street past the museum and one more block south until we come to this little tavern which looks quite old. Dr. Yorgonavich explains to me that sometimes she comes here while she's on break at the Museum. She says that I will like the food here and that it is an improvement over the MRE's that we were eating on Ice Island. Anyway we enter the tavern and are greeted by a hostess who sits us down right away. When we are seated we both order a couple of Russian beers. I look at the menu and see that it's all in Russian so I ask Dr. Yorgonavich to order what she orders and that I'm sure that I will like it.

Dr. Yorgonavich informs me that while she was in her room this afternoon she received a phone call from General Klienowski. He requested our presence at one of the meetings here close to the Kremlin. He informed Dr. Yorgonavich that it was an important meeting and that his superior would be there. This meeting is going to take place tomorrow morning at 10 am. Dr. Yorgonavich tells me that he says nothing else about the meeting. Her and I start talking about what we think should become of Ice Island. We both think that it should be protected and only scientists with special permission be allowed to go there. We both really wonder what General Klienowski and his superiors are thinking what they want to do with the island. I try asking her if she would be interested in ever going back again and she informs me with hesitation in her voice that she would. I try to change the subject because I can still see that the deaths that occurred within our group still bother her. To my surprise she asks me if I would be interested in going back to the island. I inform her that I intend to someday go back if I'm allowed.

Well finally our dinner arrives at our table and we both decide to stop talking and to start eating which is exactly what we do. The food here is delicious and I think we are both very hungry and finish our food very quickly. We order dessert and eat that as well and order a few more drinks of beer. This ends up being kind of a celebration dinner for what we just went through on Ice Island. I explain to her that I think I should call my superior Dr. Klotz back in Washington DC just to let him know that everything is okay. She takes out her cell phone and tells me that she will take care of calling him for me because she has it on her cell phone number and has a special connection to reach their. After she dials the number for me she hands me- her cell phone. After a couple rings the Secretary Ms. Gentry answers the phone and I talk to her for a couple minutes and she is very glad to hear from me. Ms. Gentry connects me through to Dr. Klotz who immediately picks up and is surprised to hear from me. I inform him that everything is okay and that I am back here in Moscow. He asks me all kinds of questions about what happened on the island and what I found. I inform him that I'm in the middle of dinner and that I will explain everything that happened to me and everything that I saw once I get back to Washington DC. I informed him that I have a very important meeting tomorrow and want to wait to see what happens at this meeting before I discuss with him anything else. He understands and asks me when I will be returning to Washington DC. I inform him that it will be the day after tomorrow. We then say goodbye and I disconnect the call and hand the phone back to Dr. Yorgonavich. We both have a couple more drinks and by the time we are finished with our dinner there at this tavern it is late. I look at my watch and it is about 9 pm we both decide to leave so that we get some sleep and get up early for this meeting tomorrow morning. Dr. Yorgonavich pays the bill and we both head outside the tavern and walk back to our hotel. Once we get back to our hotel we both head to our rooms and call it a night.

The morning hour comes very quickly and I am up by 6 am. I decide to take a nice hot shower and take my time getting ready for the meeting this morning. I put on a nice three-piece suit that I brought from the states. I am looking and feeling cleaner than I have in the past couple of weeks. I feel very refreshed and ready for this meeting. At about 8 am I decide to call Dr. Yorgonavich in her room. She immediately picks the phone up and informs me she is still getting ready for the meeting. She asks me to meet her down in the lobby of the hotel at 9 am. I hang up the phone and tidy myself up a little bit more and then head down to the lobby to eat some continental breakfast. When I get down to the lobby there's a few people there and I go grab a cup of coffee and some Russian bread that is very similar to our bagels. After approximately another hour I see Dr. Yorgonavich coming down the lobby to where I am. She looks absolutely fabulous and is in a long dress and looks very refreshed. When she comes over towards me I let her know how wonderful she looks and she says the same to me. She goes and gets a cup of coffee and then sits down next to me. Dr. Yorgonavich informs me that we will go catch a cab in front of the hotel and head towards the Kremlin to where there is a government office where we will be having this meeting at.

After we both finish our cups of coffee we head to the front of the hotel and Dr. Yorgonavich waves down a taxicab and it comes over to where we are. We get inside the taxicab and Dr. Yorgonavich talks to the driver in Russian. I believe she is telling the taxi driver the directions to where we're going to. We drive for about 20 minutes and we pull up to a big stone government building. We both get out of the taxi and Dr. Yorgonavich pays the driver and then we proceed into the government building. We enter the building and there is two Russian military guards there. Dr. Yorgonavich shows her museum ID to the guards and says a few words to them in Russian. The guards have her sign her name on a clipboard on a piece of paper and then give me the clipboard and I sign my name there as well. We then make it past the front entrance of the building and the two guards and walk down a long hallway passing many doors on both sides of us.

We finally get to this one door where Dr. Yorgonavich opens it and we both enter the room. It is a fairly big room and there are probably 50 seats with about half of them being filled with people. In the front of the room there is a large conference table that is facing the people that are seated in the audience. There is approximately 10 seats there at the conference table eight of these seats are already filled and the two empty seats happen to be for Dr. Yorgonavich and myself. I was thinking to myself that I didn't think there would be that many people here. This seems like a somewhat grand event. Dr. Yorgonavich and I proceed to the conference table and take our seats there. There is a podium that is right next to the conference table and it has a microphone set up.

General Klienowski is at the conference table where we are sitting. He is the first one to get up and go over towards the podium. He introduces himself to the audience and speaks in Russian first and then in English. He seems to be very happy and introduces everybody by name who is sitting at the conference table. He starts off by telling everyone about the discovery of this Ice Island. He then gets into very detailed explanations about what was found on the island and about the valley itself. He gives great detail and enthusiasm about explaining the discovery of woolly mammoths and some of the other creatures that were discovered there on Ice Island. You could see the people in the audience get very excited and where paying very close attention to what he was saying. He goes on to say that there has been a law made just today to protect Ice Island and nobody will be allowed on the island except by special permission from the board members sitting at this conference table in front of you with the exception of Dr. Harrison. He explains that I am the exception because I am a US citizen and cannot be on this board. He explains that anyone that wants to go to Ice Island will be voted by this Stupowski. He assures us that those pictures will be returned to Dr. Yorgonavich after his superior is done with them but could not give us an exact time or date that will happen. He just promises Dr. Yorgonavich that she will have those photos for her new exhibit there at the Museum within the next month.

General Klienowski turns to me and shakes my hand and again thanks me for all my hard work. He asks me when I will be returning to the United States. I tell him that I'm leaving tomorrow morning to return to Washington DC. He informs me that I will probably be very occupied with all the reporters from magazines and newspapers once I land there in Washington DC. He informs me the rest of the world did not know anything about Ice Island until this announcement a few minutes ago. He walks away and starts mingling. I turn to Dr. Yorgonavich and we both look at each other with excitement about having our expedition logbooks returned.

Dr. Yorgonavich asks me if I want to leave and if I would like to go back to the museum with her. I inform her I would love to get out of here and go back to the museum with her. She tells me that she's supposed to meet her assistant Evan within the next 30 minutes there at the museum.

Dr. Yorgonavich and I leave the building and jump into a taxicab that takes us back to the Moscow Museum. Once we get there we go right into the museum and towards her office. We spot her assistant Evan waiting right outside of her office. He comes right up to Dr. Yorgonavich and informs her that she received boxes of things from that expedition at Ice Island and that it is in her office. He informs us that he saw the Russian military dropping it off at her office this morning and when he asked what it was they informed him that it's things to help start up a new exhibit at the Museum.

Dr. Yorgonavich opens up her office door and sees a few boxes there and opens them up immediately. She sees the uniforms that we wore from the expedition at Ice Island along with our snowshoes. She comments to me that these will be good for the exhibit. She locks up her office door and tells her assistant Evan that she will see him tomorrow. She looks to me and asks me what I would like to do. I let her know let's go get some dinner and then I'm going to go back to my room and go to bed early and get up tomorrow and go back to Washington DC. We both walk outside and grab a taxi to take us to a nice restaurant.

We arrive to a nice restaurant on the other side of town and by this time it's 6:30 pm. We go into the restaurant and have a really nice time and talk for a couple hours and have a splendid dinner. We both had back to our hotel rooms at about 8:30 pm. She tells me good night and that she will see me to the airport tomorrow morning. I thank her and tell her I will call her in the morning when I wake up.

The next morning comes very quickly and I am up around 7:30 am. My flight leaves at 8:30 am. I call Dr. Yorgonavich in her room and she picks up and I let her know that I will meet her in the lobby in 10 minutes. Once I get downstairs to the lobby area she informs me that we better get going to the airport because there's going to be a lot of traffic. We both go outside and get into a taxicab and head to the airport. She tells me how busy she is going to be in the next couple weeks setting up this exhibit while we are driving to the airport. Well I get to the airport and she walks me out to the terminal and she gives me a hug. She tells me to give her a call once I get to Washington DC and settled in. I let her know I will do that and make my way onto the aircraft. I can see that she's really got a lot of things on her mind and so do I. There are a lot of things I have to get done once I get back to Washington DC. Everything seems to be going at such a fast pace at this time. Well I get seated inside the aircraft and after a few minutes the aircraft takes off down the runway. It looks like I'm homeward bound now. I take one last look outside the window and can see Moscow getting smaller.

CHAPTER 8
The Washington DC Return

After a brief stop in Germany and flying across the Atlantic Ocean I finally arrive in Washington DC. When I arrive it is a beautiful sunny day out. Nobody is there to greet me because nobody knew what time I was arriving there at the airport. I get into a taxi cab that takes me immediately to my apartment. Once I get inside my apartment I listen to my answering machine. On my answering machine there are three messages all from Dr. Klotz. All of his messages are urging me to contact him immediately. He explains that he heard the news about the woolly mammoths and Ice Island on the local news last night. His voice sounds very excited and he sounds like he's very intrigued in what I have to say about my expedition. In his last message on my answering machine he explains that this morning he was swamped with magazines and newspaper reporters wanting to know where I was and how I could be contacted for interviews. In this last message he left on my machine he told me to contact him immediately.

I am very jetlagged from this long flight and it is late afternoon so I decide just to eat something in my apartment and go right to sleep even though I am excited to find out what all the commotion is about these magazines and newspapers who want to interview me. I also decide not to call Dr. Klotz and feel it is better to see him in person tomorrow at the Museum. Before I go to sleep in my bed I find myself thinking about Dr. Yorgonavich and decide to call her very quickly to let her know that I arrived safely. When I call her phone number at her office at the Moscow Museum I hear a message machine pick up and it is her voice on the message machine but it is in Russian. I decide to leave a message letting her know that it was me and that I arrived safely here in Washington DC. I asked her to give me a call back when she has time. I then set my alarm clock for 7:30 am and fall asleep.

The next morning I'm awakened from my alarm clock going off. I get up and take a hot shower and make it into my kitchen and eat some breakfast. I check my cell phone to see if I have any messages on it and to my surprise I have a message from Dr. Yorgonavich telling me how sorry she was for not being able to answer her phone when I called her. She informs me how busy she's been at the Moscow Museum, and that she will give me a call later tonight.

I head out of my apartment and make my way into a taxicab which takes me to the museum. I get out at the Museum and head to my office in the basement. I sit down at my desk and make myself a fresh cup of coffee. I'm thinking to myself about how wonderful it is to be back in Washington DC and here in the United States. It's a strange feeling to be in a country where you don't speak their language. I feel much more relaxed being back here. I feel wide awake here this morning and completely over my jet lag from yesterday. I decide to wait until 9 am to go visit Dr. Klotz at his office.

I enter Dr. Klotz's office and see the secretary Miss Gentry. She immediately gets up from her desk and comes over and gives me a big hug. She congratulates me and tells me how famous I am now. She informs me how my name is all over the news about the discovery of Ice Island and the creatures that were found on it. She informs me to go right into Dr. Klotz's office and that he is waiting to hear from me.

I knock on the door and instantly enter Dr. Klotz's office. He is sitting at his desk and immediately gets up and comes over to shake my hand. I've never seen him this excited before. He asks me if I'd like a cup of coffee and I tell him no because I ·just had some in my office. He tells me I'm a celebrity here in the United States and that my name has been mentioned on all major news stations across the country. He continues to tell me that he has had a dozen calls since yesterday asking if I was available for interviews. He even told me Geographic magazine called yesterday and wants to interview me. He asks me to take a seat which I do and to tell him all about the expedition. I tell him about the expedition for about an hour and even get out my log book to give to him so he can read it. I tell him that he can get it back to me tomorrow. He talks to me about what I think about setting up an exhibit here at our museum about Ice Island. I told him I think it would be a great idea and think it would be great to talk to Dr. Yorgonavich about any ideas she could help us with for this exhibit. He then hands me a piece of paper with all of the magazines and news agencies phone numbers that want to interview me. He tells me that I am going to become a very rich man with all this money that I am going to make from these interviews. Though I know he was only half joking about becoming rich over the interviews; I still needed to let him know that the money doesn't matter to me and that the only thing that matters to me now is that Ice Island stays safe and that I get another chance to go back there and study it. He agrees with me and hopes that I do get another chance someday to go back and study it. He informs me that we have a lot to get done here at the museum for this new exhibit. He tells me to take a week off and that I could come back next Monday and start work He shakes my hand one more time and then I leave his office and head back to my office.

While I am sitting at my desk in my office I find my mind drifting off and thinking about Dr. Yorgonavich and what she is doing right now. Right at that moment my cell phone rings and to my surprise it is Dr. Yorgonavich. She's very excited to hear my voice. She tells me how busy she is setting up the exhibit at the Moscow Museum and I tell her about how Dr. Klotz wants to set up one here. She thinks that is a fabulous idea. I ask about what is going on with the board she is on and what is happening. She informs me that she is pushing hard to be able to go back again to the island and explore some more and wants to know if I am interested in going along with her. I let her know about all the interviews that I'm going to have with magazines and news agencies this week. She finds that fascinating. I tell her about how I was thinking about her and she tells me that she's been thinking about me as well. I ask her if she would be interested in coming back here to Washington so that she could interview with some of these magazines as well. She says she would love to do that and tells me she will fly there so that she can do that next week if I agree to come back to Moscow so that we can arrange for another expedition to Ice Island. I agree and we both kind of sound very excited to see each other next week. I tell her I'll give her a call tomorrow and we both say goodbye and hang up.

To my amazement I felt a special connection with Dr. Yorgonavich that I don't think I've ever felt with anybody else. I'm hoping that she kind of feels that special connection between us as well. Well tomorrow it looks like I'll start contacting these magazines and news agencies for interviews. My mind wanders back to Ice Island and what the whole expedition meant. I'm still trying to figure all this out. The one thing that I do hope for is that the Woolly Creatures of such a unique place continue to exist and I will do all I can to ensure this.

www.ingramcontent.com/pod-product-compliance
Lightning Source LLC
Chambersburg PA
CBHW022032170626
46808CB00003B/1164